ONE BRAVE SUMMER

D1318331

ONE BRAVE SUMMER

**Kiersi Burkhart and
Amber J. Keyser**

darbycreek

MINNEAPOLIS

Darby Creek
A division of Lerner Publishing Group, Inc.
241 First Avenue North
Minneapolis, MN 55401 USA

For reading levels and more information, look up this title at www.lernerbooks.com.

The images in this book are used with the permission of: © iStockphoto.com/Piotr Krześlak (wood background).

Front cover: © Barbara O'Brien Photography.
Back cover: © iStockphoto.com/ImagineGolf

Main body text set in Bembo Std regular 12.5/17.
Typeface provided by Monotype Typography.

Library of Congress Cataloging-in-Publication Data

Names: Burkhart, Kiersi, author. | Keyser, Amber, author.
Title: One brave summer / by Kiersi Burkhart and Amber J. Keyser.
Description: Minneapolis : Darby Creek, [2017] | Series: Quartz Creek Ranch |
    Summary: "To learn to ride Prince, gamer Paley is forced to identify her real-life
    powers. But her newfound courage will be tested when ranch neighbors threaten to
    steal an exciting discovery"— Provided by publisher.
Identifiers: LCCN 2016015781 (print) | LCCN 2016028416 (ebook) |
    ISBN 9781467792547 (th : alk. paper) | ISBN 9781512430882 (pb : alk. paper) |
    ISBN 9781512408928 (eb pdf)
Subjects: | CYAC: Ranch life—Fiction. | Horses—Fiction. | Friendship—Fiction. |
    Fossils—Fiction. | African Americans—Fiction.
Classification: LCC PZ7.1.B88 On 2017 (print) | LCC PZ7.1.B88 (ebook) | DDC
    [Fic]—dc23

LC record available at https://lccn.loc.gov/2016015781

Manufactured in the United States of America
1-38282-20007-8/24/2016

For all the strong, brave horses who have left a hoofprint in my life: you spotted beauties, all of you.

—**K.B.**

For Beryl, my favorite horse girl.

—**A.K.**

CHAPTER ONE

Paley Dixon had almost earned enough gold to buy a dragon's egg. All she had to do was accomplish three more tasks for the Elder Mage, and she would be on her way to Glendel Cave. The light from the screen illuminated her face as she spun the wheel on the mouse and directed the Blue Elf toward the Misery Marshes.

Paley had stayed up all night to get this far. Outside, the sun began to climb in the sky. In-game it was dusk, and the Blue Elf was on the move. Reeds rustled against her leather pants. Gold coins in the pouch at her thigh rattled. On the other side of Paley's bedroom door, she heard steps. Her mother, no doubt, pausing to fret at Paley's door before moving on to wake up Paley's nine-year-old brother in the next room.

Paley reached for her headphones without taking her eyes from the screen to block out the loud noise her brother would be making soon. This part of the game was tricky. There were fire snakes.

The Elder Mage, a tall, copper-skinned man with a hooked nose and a mane of silver hair, held out a piece of parchment. The Blue Elf took it in her slender, dark fingers and read the message—*Retrieve twelve hairs from the tail of a golden fox*. The elf bowed, her blue hair like a waterfall. She swept it back and turned away from the Mage and toward Paley.

The graphics were so real that Paley thought she caught the Blue Elf wink at her, one sky-blue eye in a face as dark as night. Paley winked back as if the Blue Elf were her own reflection, even though her own eyes and skin were brown and her real-life ears were definitely not pointy.

Then the Blue Elf was off again, muscles rippling, as she raced across the Misery Marshes.

Paley reached for a bag of chips. Empty. She balled the foil and tossed it to the floor. There was no time to stop for food. The faster she got those fox hairs, the closer she'd be to her dragon.

Light flooded her room as her dad flipped on the switch and pulled the cord on the mini blind. "It's time to go."

Paley squinted against the brightness as she scrabbled at the keyboard. "Can't. Got to finish. So close."

"Paley," he said, "shut down the game."

"Just a second!" she screeched, sounding way too goblin, even to herself.

Her dad picked up the potato chip wrapper. It crinkled as he threw it in the trash. "The car is loaded."

"I have to finish this quest!"

"We have to drop your brother off at his friend's house and hit the road." He leaned over and turned off the computer.

Paley roared, more cave troll rumble than goblin shriek this time. "You can't do that!"

"I can and I did. It's time to go," he repeated, plucking the headphones off her head.

She slammed the mouse on the desk and refused to look at him. He watched her without speaking for a long time. She glared at the blank screen.

"You agreed to this."

"Only because it was better than stupid basket-ball camp."

Her dad's eyes narrowed, and his nose pinched together like he'd stumbled into a stench pit in the Misery Marshes. "We've been through this, Paley. You can't stay in this dark room playing video games forever. You've got to make an effort."

She spun her desk chair around so she wouldn't have to look at him.

Moving from Los Angeles to Denver right before starting middle school had been awful. Her parents thought she hadn't tried to make friends, but she had.

At least at first.

But all the kids already knew one another from fifth grade and were into stuff like skiing and cyclocross. It didn't help that she was one of the only black kids at school. The Blue Elf had better things to do than suck up to a bunch of obnoxious brats, and it wasn't like she expected seventh grade to be any better. Right now, all Paley wanted was the summer.

The whole summer.

To lose herself in the world of *Dragonfyre*, the place where she could accomplish anything.

"Hey, you two!" Paley's mom leaned into the room, her smile as forced as her cheery tone. "Horses are waiting!"

"Maybe *you* should go to camp, then," Paley muttered.

Her parents exchanged a worried glance.

Paley wished she was a snot-dripping cave troll so she could toss them out of the way and get back to finding those fox hairs. As far as Paley could tell, the only good thing about getting banished to a horse ranch in the middle of nowhere for six weeks was that she wouldn't have to listen to her parents lecture her about reaching out and finding new interests.

The Blue Elf wouldn't let anyone push her around like this, but Paley Dixon wasn't the Blue Elf, and her parents were pulling the plug.

\\\

Paley made a point of not speaking for the entire drive from Denver to Quartz Creek Ranch. With every mile, the dragon's egg slipped further out of reach. The stupid camp they were sending her to didn't allow technology. It was practically child abuse.

In the front seat, her parents tuned in country music. In the back, Paley alternated between glowering out the window and studying the big, glossy book of game art from *Dragonfyre* cradled in her lap.

As they left the city and the suburbs far behind and began to climb into the mountains, Paley lingered on the pages with horses.

Armored stallions stamped their gilded hooves, and the vampire horses dripped blood from their sharp fangs. Best of all were the winged mares that shot through the sky like comets. If the Blue Elf couldn't have a dragon, Paley wanted one of those, especially if it breathed fire.

It was nearly lunchtime by the time they drove through the town of Quartz Creek. Paley closed the book and stared at the cutesy shops that lined Main Street. A sign in the window of the local rock shop read *Rock My World!* The candy store proclaimed *Taffy Making on Fridays!*

Paley felt like she was in a cautionary after-school TV special. *Troubled kid from LA goes to horse camp and everything turns out roses and cupcakes.*

Her stomach growled. If only she could conjure a cupcake.

A few blocks down the road, she spied a comic book shop. That was promising.

If they ever let her into town.

Main Street was so short that five minutes later, they had passed all the way through town. It seemed to Paley that a single city block in LA could swallow all of dinky old Quartz Creek, Colorado.

After just a few more minutes, her dad turned onto a dirt road and they were passing under a metal arch that read QUARTZ CREEK RANCH. Paley wished she could teleport back to LA. Still, she couldn't help plastering her face against the car window. A stream tumbled alongside the dirt road. Velvety-green horse pastures rolled away into the hills on either side.

And oh, the horses!

Even a cave troll could get excited about animals like these. White ones like cloud fluff. A gray one spotted with stars. Brown ones that looked like cinnamon and caramel and chocolate and everything good.

Her dad parked the car next to a big ranch house with a wide front porch and huge windows facing the mountains to the west. That felt right to Paley. When she played *Dragonfyre*, she always remembered to face west when spell-casting. Ignoring the cardinal directions on the game map always caused magic to backfire.

Paley got out of the car and stretched. The smell of newly cut grass and the sound of birds enveloped her. The heavy, horrible weight of the last year at school felt a little lighter. Maybe she could stop being a cave troll after all. Paley frowned. It was a classic *Dragonfyre* trap. Just when you thought that you were home free, the goblins always came roaring down on you. No one was going to catch her with her guard down.

Paley squinted against the sun and scrutinized the ranch.

Near the big house were two little cabins with porches. A split-rail fence ran along the edge of the gravel parking area. Horses dotted the pasture. On the other side of the creek was a big barn and an outdoor riding arena filled with kids and horses.

Paley had almost forgotten that there would be other kids here. She couldn't believe her parents thought she belonged with a bunch of troublemakers. Being a gamer wasn't a problem! *No, it's not*, her mom had said. *But being online every waking moment is.* Paley kicked her toes in the gravel.

Up on the porch, her parents were talking in that super-serious, worried-parent way with an older couple. Paley ignored them and climbed up one rung of the fence to look at the horses. Three of them grazed placidly. They were lovely but definitely not fierce. If she was going to learn how to joust this summer, she needed a much bigger mount.

The thundering of hooves brought her back to reality.

From far off in the pasture came a huge horse in full gallop. It raced across the field, scattering the other horses. Its coat was black as midnight, and its muscles rippled, sleek as a panther. At the top of a small rise, it stopped, surveying its realm before sauntering toward her. A hundred feet from Paley, it tossed its head and neighed.

Paley almost jumped out of her skin with excitement.

This was a storybook horse. The perfect steed to carry the Blue Elf into battle.

All around the horse, the sunlight gleamed and sparkled. It was so dazzling, Paley wouldn't have been surprised if it had unfurled wings.

"Well, Paley, what do you think?" The older woman who had been talking to her parents leaned over the fence and tilted her head toward the huge black horse. She had curly gray hair and was wearing Wranglers and a T-shirt that said *My Other Car Is a Horse.*

"Magnificent!" Paley said, mesmerized by the way the horse's coat shone blue-black in the sun.

The older man joined them at the fence. "Don't

let Prince hear you call him *magnificent*. He's already got a big head," he said, chuckling.

"His name is Prince?" asked Paley, looking up at the tall, stern-faced man with dark, coppery skin.

"Yes, indeed, little lady." He tipped his cowboy hat, revealing short, salt-and-pepper hair. "And I'm Willard Bridle. This here is Ma Etty. We're glad to have you at the ranch." His voice was low and slow, and he smelled like bacon and coffee.

Paley squinted up at him. Mr. Bridle reminded her of the Elder Mage. Minus the long, silver hair, of course. Switch out the jeans and flannel for some robes and—presto! It was easy to imagine Mr. Bridle sitting around a fire practicing spells.

"I never get tired of horses," said Ma Etty, leaning over the fence. "I could watch them forever." In-game, Ma Etty would be a healer with a bag full of herbs and maybe a dried newt or two.

"I can't wait to ride," said Paley, unable to contain the dazzling feeling Prince had sparked in her.

Ma Etty laughed, and the wrinkles around her eyes crinkled up in a happy way. "This one's perfect for us, isn't she, Mr. Bridle?"

"Indeed," he said. "After lunch, I'll have Fletch

bring Mr. Magnificent into the barn so you two can get acquainted."

"Wait. What?" Paley glanced between the couple. "I get to ride Prince?" She could already see herself on his back, racing the wind.

The old woman slung her arm around Paley's shoulders. "He's your horse all summer."

"Really?" Paley gasped. It was like stumbling upon a treasure cache, unexpected and unearned.

"You betcha!" Ma Etty laughed. She was short, only a little taller than Paley, but way more fit. The year of cave trolling had left Paley pudgy and out of shape, but she didn't try to shake off the old woman's squeeze. All the healers were kind people.

Unlike her parents.

Paley scowled at them as they finished unloading her duffel bag from the car.

"All right, then," said her mom, clasping her hands in front of her. "I guess this is good-bye."

"We'll take good care of her," said Mr. Bridle.

"And no computers, right?" her father prompted.

"No computers, no cell phones. Usually folks can't find a signal out here anyway. We do have one computer, but it's used for work and research. That's it," Ma Etty assured him.

Paley backed away from Ma Etty. So much for the old lady being a kind and helpful healer. Her parents shook hands with the Bridles and said stupid, fakey things and shot worried glances her way, but all Paley could think about was how much this summer was going to suck.

No computer.

No game.

No Blue Elf.

Even a horse like Prince couldn't save her now.

CHAPTER TWO

Paley didn't bother to watch her parents leave. She'd had enough of *This is for your own good* and *You need some good, old-fashioned outside time*. First they forced her to leave LA. Now this.

"Let's eat. I'm starving," said Ma Etty, leading the way toward the back of the big house. A fluffy, white hen waddled in front of her. "Don't worry, Marshmallow. You're not on the menu."

Paley looked up. "Are you talking to that chicken?"

Ma Etty laughed again, and three more chickens came running toward the sound of her voice. "You bet I am. These are my babies."

Mr. Bridle chuckled. "She names them all after food."

"Seriously?" Paley couldn't believe these two. Since when were old people so . . . so . . . goofy?

"That's Dumpling, Hot Tamale, and Pat o' Butter," said Ma Etty, pointing to each hen in turn. "But they are all layers, not broilers. You could help me collect eggs, if you'd like, one of these days."

"No, thanks." Paley shoved her hands in her pockets. Chicken eggs were a poor substitute for dragon eggs.

Paley followed the Bridles up the back porch steps. Mr. Bridle held the door open for them, and Ma Etty ushered Paley inside the big screened porch like another one of her chickens. "Leave your boots here, honey."

Various hats and coats hung from a row of hooks. Muck boots, cowboy boots, sneakers, and a very beat-up pair of fluffy slippers were lined up near the door. Paley left her scuffed, hand-me-down cowboy boots next to a pair of fancy knee-high riding boots.

She slipped on sock feet down a wide hallway. The first room on the left was an office. Paley paused at the open door, which had a sign taped to it: *Internal Affairs*. The work-only computer sat in the middle of a desk covered with open ledgers, stacks of official-looking documents, and several newspapers.

That was a waste of a perfectly good Internet connection.

Paley slumped after Ma Etty into a big, sunny kitchen. A girl with strawberry blonde hair was laying out sandwich fixings. She wore pristine riding clothes—tan jodhpurs and a pressed white blouse.

"Well, look at you, Leila!" said Ma Etty. "You've prepped everything. Thanks!" The girl grinned at her. Ma Etty introduced Paley and urged them to make their sandwiches before the rest of the crew showed up.

"How was your morning lesson?" Ma Etty asked Leila as she slathered mayo on bread.

"Best ever."

"That's something, given how much riding you've done, missy."

"Cupcake is such a sweet horse."

Ma Etty pulled down a stack of plates. "Wait until you see her play soccer."

"Soccer?" asked Paley and Leila together.

"You betcha!" Ma Etty's eyes twinkled. "Ask Madison to show you one of these days."

"Show 'em what?" A pretty, college-aged girl with long, dark hair and bangs followed them into the kitchen. "Just what are you signing me up for,

Ma Etty?" She stuck out her hand toward Paley, who shook it. "I'm Madison, one of your trainers. You must be Paley."

"Ma Etty said that Cupcake plays soccer," Leila said, finding a place at the table. "Will you show me later?"

"Absolutely," said Madison. "It's a total kick in the pants."

The kitchen was filling up with kids.

One was a beefy white kid named Bryce who sported spiked blond hair and wore jeans and a plaid shirt. He grunted, cut in front of Paley, and fixed himself two ginormous sandwiches with every kind of meat.

Another girl stood behind Paley in the sandwich line. She had dark skin and sparkly eyes and was dressed in fancy riding clothes like Leila. "Hi, I'm Sundee. I like your braid."

Paley's hand went to her hair. She usually wore a thick braid to keep her hair out of her way. "Thanks."

Sundee made herself a cheese sandwich. "I'm vegetarian," she explained when she caught Paley watching. Behind Sundee, another boy with lots of freckles and a mop of curly brown hair stepped up to assemble his lunch. His face was red and sweaty.

Paley found a seat and ate her sandwich in silence, studying the other kids. The girls seemed nice enough, but both were good riders. You could just tell from their clothes. In-game, they'd be archers, Paley decided. Leila looked like she'd be a crack shot.

Ma Etty clinked a fork against her glass of lemonade. The buzz of conversation around the big table quieted. "You've probably noticed," Ma Etty began, "that we've got a new face at the table." She smiled broadly at Paley, who ducked her chin as every head turned her way. "Paley wasn't able to make it last night for introductions, so how 'bout a quick repeat? Let's go around the table and say our names and one thing we like to do for fun. Mr. Bridle, you're first."

The tall, old man ran his fingers through his graying hair. "I'm Willard Bridle." His voice was low and liquid. "And currently I'm interested in genealogy, Paiute ancestry on my grandmother's side, in particular." He was Elder Mage for sure.

"That sounds fun," Bryce muttered.

"My name is Cameron," said the sweaty-faced boy. "I like dirt bikes and books with sword-fighting and stuff." Paley could totally see him as a blacksmith's apprentice, pounding out blades in front of a fiery forge.

Bryce smirked.

"Hey, I'm a reader too," said a blond, middle-aged guy sitting next to Cameron. "I'm Paul, the ranch manager. I write cowboy poetry." He grinned at Paley and pretended to tip an imaginary hat. Leila liked to play Frisbee with her dog. Sundee collected rocks. Madison's favorite thing to do was swim.

When it was Paley's turn, she said, "I like to play *Dragonfyre*."

Bryce laughed out loud. "That game is so gay." Paley wished she could stomp him flat, cave troll style.

Ma Etty touched his shoulder. "All right, Bryce, we don't use that word as an insult here."

He twitched away from her hand. "Whatever."

"Paley, you'll have to tell me about that game when we've got some free time," said Ma Etty. Paley bit her lip and nodded. "Bryce," Ma Etty continued as if nothing had happened, "what do you like to do for fun?"

He rolled his shoulders back and puffed out his chest. Paley edged her chair away from him. What a bully. If he played *Dragonfyre*, he'd probably run around torching villages for fun.

"I like remote-control airplanes, and I'm on the swim team."

Paley gave him a second look, surprised. If she'd thought about it, Paley might have expected him to say football or wrestling. Remote-control anything was cool.

Madison gave him the thumbs up. "Swimmers unite!"

He didn't exactly smile back, but his scowl faded.

"Excellent," said Ma Etty. "And welcome, Paley. We are super-glad you're here. I stand by two things, which I said last night, and I'm saying again. Number one: *Everyone starts fresh at Quartz Creek Ranch*. And number two: *Horses make everything better*."

"Hear, hear!" said Paul with gusto, and Madison clapped.

Paley chewed her sandwich in silence. According to her parents, moving to Denver had been a "fresh start" and a "new opportunity." In reality, it had turned out to be a disaster, and she didn't expect much more from the summer. But then she thought of Prince and the way he raced across the pasture, and a flush of anticipation filled her.

Maybe, just maybe, it would be okay.

\\\

After lunch, Ma Etty assigned chores. Sundee and Leila went to the garden to pull weeds. Cameron and Bryce had dish duty. Mr. Bridle and Paul were going to the feed store in town.

"As for you, Paley," said Ma Etty, over the clamor of Bryce slamming utensils in the dishwasher, "you get to spend some quality time with Prince."

"How come she doesn't have chores?" Bryce complained.

"Here at the ranch I try to make sure everyone ends up doing what they need to do," said Ma Etty.

"And I need dishes?"

"You do if you want to eat again tonight."

Bryce was still grumbling when Ma Etty handed Paley two sandwiches wrapped in waxed paper and sent her out to the barn. "These are for Fletch, our other trainer. He missed lunch."

Paley pulled on her boots and walked around the house. She stopped to watch a fluffy yellow hen and a scrappy red one play tug-of-war with a worm.

"Ma Etty calls that red one Hot Tamale because she's so feisty," said a tall, black teenager about the same color as her. "Howdy. I'm Fletch." He touched the brim of his cowboy hat. "Welcome to QCR."

He stuck out his hand, and Paley shook it, trying not to gape at his muscled arms. He was handsome, in a sad-eyed kind of way.

"Here's your lunch."

"Great, thanks. Let's get you set up grooming Prince before I eat." He gestured Paley into the dim interior of the barn. Hay dust tickled Paley's nose, and birds rustled in the rafters. "Tack room's in here."

She followed Fletch into a room full of horse stuff—saddles, ropes, bridles, brushes, and other things she didn't recognize. It smelled like leather and oil and horse.

"Find a helmet that fits." He pointed to a rack on one wall. "You don't need it this afternoon, but you might as well be prepared for tomorrow. We have lessons every morning, then ranch chores after lunch. After that you've got free time."

Paley tried on several helmets, found one that seemed right, and clipped the helmet strap under her chin.

"Do you wear a helmet?" she asked Fletch.

"When I'm bronc riding, I do. It looks dorky. But concussion? No, thank you." He checked the fit on her helmet, made a few adjustments, and then nodded his approval.

"I didn't know there were black cowboys," she said.

"You mean you've never heard of George Fletcher?" The trainer shook his head like she'd said that she had never heard of the moon.

Paley shrugged her shoulders. "Sorry."

"Well, you should look him up," he said, handing her a red plastic tote with a handle in the middle and compartments on either side for a variety of combs, brushes, and picks. "I borrowed my nickname from George Fletcher. The guy was an extraordinary horseman. Rode saddle broncs. They called him the People's Champion."

He put a couple of scoops of sweet-smelling grain into a bucket and led Paley to an empty stall. The nameplate on the door said *Prince* in big letters. "Leave the grooming tote, hang your helmet on that hook, and grab his lead rope and halter," he said. "We'll go get Prince out of the pasture."

Paley took the thick red rope and halter and followed Fletch outside.

"The great thing about horses," he continued, "is that they don't care about the color of your skin or how expensive your riding boots are. They respond to what's in here." Fletch patted his chest right over his heart. "Confidence. Conviction. Courage. That's what Mr. Bridle always says."

Great. Paley was pretty sure she'd come up empty on all three, but she plodded after Fletch. At the pasture gate, he stopped and shook the bucket. All the horses stopped grazing to look at him. Up on the hill, Prince high-stepped and held his head to the sky.

"What a show-off," said Fletch, but he was smiling as he watched the horse prance this way and that. The mares couldn't decide who was more interesting, the trainer with the grain or Prince. Paley imagined Prince in armor, stamping the ground with his hooves. If the Blue Elf had a horse like that, she could conquer anything.

Suddenly, the magnificent horse raised his head and looked straight at her. Straight *into* her. A burst of energy surged through Paley as if there were a shimmering golden thread that connected them.

The Elder Mage spoke of such things, of the way two beings could be entwined. It was the highest form of magic.

Paley's heart leaped.

This was *her* horse for the next six weeks.

His name was Prince.

CHAPTER THREE

"**A**re you okay?" Fletch asked, touching her shoulder.

In an instant the electric feeling was gone, and she was regular old Paley Dixon once again.

"Yeah," she said, "I'm fine. Now what?"

Fletch grinned. "It's horse time."

When they were twenty feet away from Prince, the horse turned toward them.

"Hello, Your Majesty," said Paley.

As if he understood, the big black horse tossed his head so that his mane whipped around, movie star style.

Paley couldn't help laughing. "He thinks he's all that, doesn't he?"

"Yes, he does," said Fletch, holding out the bucket so that Prince could nibble grain.

Up close, Prince was even bigger than Paley had realized. Her head barely came up to his back. When she stroked his nose, she'd never felt anything softer. His coat was black velvet and his mane glistened.

"Let him smell the halter," said Fletch. She held it up, and the big horse sniffed more delicately than she thought possible. "Good," the trainer continued. "Now slide it up over his nose. The buckle clasps by his cheek."

Paley had to stand on tiptoes to get the halter adjusted properly. When she was done, Fletch had her attach the lead rope under Prince's chin. She held it while Fletch opened the gate.

As they waited, Prince snuffled and nudged her shoulder with his nose.

"What's he doing?" Paley asked.

"He's checking you out," said Fletch. "Everything you do around a horse tells him about you. The way you breathe. The way you walk. The way you feel. He knows."

Paley ran her hand down the length of Prince's neck.

What a horse! If she could ride him . . . if he would let her . . . on his back, she would be way more like the Blue Elf than a cave troll. It would be like *Dragonfyre*—but real! She could hardly keep from squealing.

Fletch led Prince into the aisle of the barn. "These are cross-ties," he said, indicating short ropes attached to eyebolts on either side of the aisle. "They clip on either side of Prince's halter. You do the left one."

Once Prince was secure, Fletch held out a round brush with stiff rubber bristles. "This is a curry comb. Make small circles to dislodge dirt and hair." He demonstrated on Prince's shoulder. "I'll get you a mounting block so you can reach his back."

When he returned with the small step-stool, Paley was already working her way down Prince's neck.

"You're doing great. He likes that. After the curry comb, use the brush with the stiff bristles to sweep away the dirt. I'm going to muck out Sawbones's stall."

"Is that your horse?"

"Well, the Bridles own him, but yeah, he's mine."

Fletch smiled so wide that even his eyes didn't look sad anymore.

Paley went back to grooming Prince. She made sure to get out every chunk of mud and all the loose hairs. It was mesmerizing to brush him. Paley snuffled at Prince, an experiment in talking horse. He snuffled back. She leaned into Prince and closed her eyes as she swept the brush down his gleaming flank. She could imagine the two of them galloping across the Misery Marshes. She'd lean low on his neck, velvet cloak streaming out behind her. When the roar of the goblin army rose behind them, she'd rise up in the stirrups, fit an arrow to her bow, and—

"What the heck are you doing?"

The question from out of nowhere startled Paley, and she nearly fell off the mounting block. Prince sidestepped and came up tight against one of the cross-ties. Paley caught her balance and stared at the girl she'd first met in the kitchen.

"Sorry," Leila said, tilting her head to one side like she was trying to figure Paley out. "I didn't mean to sneak up on you."

"I thought you were weeding," said Paley.

Leila's nose crinkled, making the smattering of

freckles across her face dance. "We did the toma-toes. Smell my hands." Her palm was smudged with pollen. Paley leaned closer. The spicy, fresh smell of crushed tomato leaves filled her nose. "Sundee is picking some for dinner. Fresh mozzarella, basil, and tomato salad. Yum! Anyway," Leila continued, "I thought you might be doing horse yoga or horse massage or something kooky."

"Horse massage?" Paley asked.

"Yeah. Ma Etty says it's a thing." The girl wiped her hands on her spotless jodhpurs, leaving a green smear. "If my mom knew how woo-woo this place is, she'd flip. She's an anesthesiologist. Very serious. About everything. Want help?"

Not really, thought Paley, but she held out the grooming tote.

Leila took a brush with extra-soft bristles and began to work loose the dried mud on Prince's legs. Paley watched her squatting there next to those huge hooves. It looked scary, but the girl seemed as at home with Prince as Paley felt playing *Dragonfyre*, like it was in her blood.

"He's a gorgeous horse," said the girl. "What's his name?"

"Prince."

The girl smiled at her.

"Do people really massage horses?" Paley asked.

Leila shrugged. "Apparently. Can I braid his mane?"

Oh man. This was getting worse and worse. She'd probably make him look totally dorky. "I guess so," said Paley, reaching for a comb she could use on Prince's tail.

She gathered the thick black hair of his tail in one hand and tugged the comb through the snarls. Immediately Prince shifted his feet and twisted toward her.

"Don't stand right behind him," Leila said. Paley dropped the tail and jumped away like she'd been bitten. "He can't see you," Leila explained, in a voice that made it clear Paley should have known that. "He's got a blind spot directly in front and directly behind."

"He's blind?" Paley couldn't believe something was wrong with her perfect horse.

Leila quirked one eyebrow up at her. "He's not blind. That's just how horse eyes work. They see to the sides, not straight ahead."

"Oh."

Leila dropped the strand of mane she had and

walked to the back of Prince, running one hand all along his body. "When I do this, he knows I'm here." She stood to one side, swept his tail into her hand, and held it out from his body to comb through it. "See? It's easy."

Paley scuffed her boot along the dusty floor. Yeah, she could see it was easy—for Leila. The last thing Paley wanted was to look stupid in front of this girl who knew everything about horses. She took back the comb. By the time she'd finished getting the knots out, Leila had worked some crazy magic on Prince's mane, which now looked like a series of perfect little roses.

Fletch returned from the far end of the barn pushing a wheelbarrow full of manure. "Better get Prince back in his stall, girls."

"Get his lead rope, and I'll get the stall door," said Leila, tossing the combs and brushes back in the grooming tote.

Paley fidgeted with the thick red rope in her hands. Prince looked askance at her, like he knew she didn't have a clue what she was doing. Paley sidled up to his left side, but Prince turned his head away. Paley tried the other side. Same problem. The cross-ties held Prince in place, but he seemed to sense her nervousness, sidestepping against the ropes.

"Don't dance around him," Leila said.

Paley's face turned hot, and she was breaking out in a sweat. The golden thread connecting her and Prince had vanished. Or maybe it had never been there at all. How was she supposed to get this horse into a stall if she couldn't even get him to stand still long enough to clip on the rope?

"Take a step back, Paley." Fletch tilted the now-empty wheelbarrow up against the barn wall and walked over to Prince. "Steady there," he said, stroking the horse's neck.

His ears pricked forward, and Paley could feel the change in him immediately. With deft hands, Fletch clasped the lead rope to Prince's halter and unclipped the cross-ties. "Remember, he feels what you feel and will respond to your confidence."

In spite of the stuffy heat of the barn, Paley felt like ice water was trickling down her back. She couldn't do this.

She just couldn't.

But the trainer put the lead rope in her sweaty hand.

Prince went shifty, his head swinging from Fletch to Leila and back to Paley.

"Come on," Paley said, walking forward and tugging on the rope. Prince didn't move. "Come on," she repeated.

"Click your tongue at him," Leila suggested. But when Paley tried it, the sound came out slobbery instead of clicky. Leila demonstrated, and Prince fixed his eyes on her.

Paley tried again and tugged on Prince. Nothing.

Leila started to offer more advice, but Fletch silenced her. "Paley can do this." To Paley, he said, "Hold the lead a little closer to his nose. Don't look at him. Look the direction you want to go."

Paley stared at the opening of the stall, willing Prince to walk in there, praying for some connection between them.

Nothing.

She held out the rope to Fletch. "I can't."

Instead of taking over, Fletch stood next to her and wrapped his hand around hers on the lead rope. He made a low clucking sound and nudged Paley forward. Prince followed like a dream. Right into the stall. Fletch unclipped the lead, closed the door, and looped the rope on a hook by Prince's stall.

"He's a good horse," said Fletch. "You'll figure him out."

Paley couldn't meet his eyes. She had already figured Prince out. Just like those girls in Denver, he didn't need her and didn't like her. She'd been wrong to expect anything else.

CHAPTER FOUR

Paley plodded after Leila as she crossed the foot-bridge over Quartz Creek and walked toward the two bunkhouses. The boys shared one small cabin with Fletch, and the girls got the other.

When Paley's parents had dropped her off before lunch, she had only had time to toss her duffel bag on one of the two bunk beds. This was her chance to unpack. Madison and Sundee were playing cards at the small table. When Paley and Leila entered, Madison flashed a big smile. "What did you think of Prince?"

"He should be on a calendar," said Leila.

"I know, right? He is one handsome horse," said Madison. "And tricky too. One time Paul was mending the fence, and he left his truck in the pasture. Prince found a bag of grain in the back of the truck and helped himself." Madison shuffled the deck of cards and kept talking. "Mr. Bridle calls Prince his backup horse. Of course, he's got about five of those."

Leila and Sundee cracked up.

Paley unzipped her duffel and began unloading. Sundee had claimed a top bunk. Leila's things were strewn across the twin bed near the window. She was pretty messy for someone who looked so perfect.

"We left you the top drawer," said Leila, pointing to the dresser on one wall. "And you have this shelf here for your little stuff. There's a spot for you in the bathroom, too."

"Thanks," said Paley. She piled her clothes into the drawer and lined up her books, the Totoro flashlight, and an Altoids tin full of barrettes on the shelf.

She sat on the bed and stared at her empty hands. They itched for a keyboard and mouse. This whole ranch thing was too much. She wasn't a bad kid. She didn't belong here. Paley snuck a look at the other girls. Sundee was dealing Leila in for a new game of gin rummy. They looked nice enough, but Paley couldn't help wondering what they'd done to end up here. She tucked her hands into her armpits and let her chin slump on her chest. She wouldn't have caused her parents any trouble this summer. All she needed was *Dragonfyre,* and everything would have been fine.

Madison sat down next to her, smelling faintly of chlorine. She was a swimmer, Paley remembered, and had the strong arms and shoulders to prove it.

"How did it go with Prince?" Madison asked.

Paley shook her head. "He doesn't like me."

"Pshaw!" Madison waved off Paley's words and put on a posh British accent. "He's a bit of a snob. That's all. We'll whip him into shape."

"I don't know anything about horses."

Madison patted her knee. "I hope not!" Paley looked at her, surprised. That made no sense. "If you knew a lot," the trainer continued, "I wouldn't get to teach you, and that wouldn't be much fun for me, would it?"

"Uh . . . I don't know."

Madison laughed. "Well, I do. Learning to ride is the best thing ever, and Prince is a superstar. You'll see." She stood and surveyed the bunkhouse. "Ladies, we have neglected a very important duty."

"I hate cleaning," Leila blurted. All eyes flew to her bed.

"We can see that," said Sundee, laying down three queens.

Madison made a show of pulling the door to her room shut as if she had an even bigger mess to hide. "We need a cabin name," she announced. "It's a ranch tradition, and the boys are way ahead of us."

"What did they pick?" asked Sundee.

"Rainbow Pony Snipers."

Even Paley had to laugh. That was a ridiculous name. No doubt Bryce had suggested the sniper part. That seemed right up his alley.

"How about the Horse Girls?" said Sundee.

Paley tried not to wince. "Maybe something a little tougher sounding?"

"Like what?" Sundee sounded miffed.

"Dragon Riders? Goblin Slayers?"

Sundee and Leila both frowned at her.

"Okay. Maybe not."

"You don't have to decide right now," said Madison, "but think about it."

Sundee looked like a squirrel contemplating a nut. "Panda Bears? Cupcake Cowgirls?"

Leila pretended to gag.

"How do you know so much about horses?" Paley asked her, still thinking about the easy way Prince had responded to Leila.

Leila shrugged. "I've been riding forever. Doing shows and stuff." Paley could practically see Leila's room with the walls covered in those big satin ribbons. No wonder her riding clothes were so fancy. "To tell you the truth," Leila continued, "competition stopped being fun a long time ago. My mom is big on winning. Real big."

Paley wondered what it would be like to be able to ride like that. The only thing she was good at was playing the Blue Elf, and that wasn't a skill anyone seemed to appreciate. No satin ribbons on her walls for gaming prowess.

While the other girls continued to suggest cabin names, Paley retreated onto her bunk with the book of *Dragonfyre* game art she'd brought with her. She loved the way the Bog Queen's green hair streamed behind her in the water and how her eyes seemed to burn deep down inside. If only she were in Greensward with the Queen chasing fairies, instead of here, where she most definitely did not belong.

\\

After dinner, everyone gathered in the living room of the big house. Paley drummed her fingers against her thigh. Sundee and Leila were doing a one-thousand-piece puzzle. The box was propped up on one side of the coffee table and showed five white horses galloping in the surf on some tropical beach. Judging from their progress, the girls would be lucky to finish it by the end of the summer. They hadn't even completed all the edges.

Cameron had his nose in a book.

Mr. Bridle and Ma Etty were reading the newspaper.

Madison and Bryce had driven to town to swim laps.

Paley checked her watch. Almost eight o'clock. At home, she'd be in her room playing *Dragonfyre*. At home, she'd have something to do. She fiddled with the remote control for the TV. "Can we watch something?" she asked.

Ma Etty pulled her reading glasses down to the tip of her nose. "We use that for movie night on Saturdays," she said. "Otherwise it stays off."

Paley put the remote down.

"Do you want to play cribbage?" Ma Etty asked.

"I don't know how."

"I'll show you."

"No, thanks." Shoving little pins in holes did not count as a game. That was just dumb.

Paley excused herself to go to the bathroom and detoured down the back hallway. The door to the office was ajar. The screen saver on the computer was a slide show of horses, some running, some working, some just standing around looking horsey.

Paley stepped into the doorway, drawn to the computer. It was old but not that old. It might be able to handle *Dragonfyre*. All she would have to do is download the program and enter her password. They didn't really expect her to go all summer without even a glimpse of the Blue Elf, did they?

She was halfway to the computer when the back door opened, and Madison and Bryce came in. "That was fun," said Madison. "You've got a great backstroke."

"Thanks," said Bryce, walking past the office door without looking in.

But Madison caught her eye and stopped.

"What are you doing?" she asked, leaning against the door frame.

"Uh . . . I was watching the screen saver. Awesome horses, huh?"

"I guess so." Madison looked at Paley like she could see right inside her head. "But no kids in the office, okay?"

Paley nodded and followed Madison to the living room. The Blue Elf fizzled back into cyberspace. Unreachable. She plopped on the couch and pretended to read an issue of *Western Horseman*. Inside she was going crazy. This was going to be the longest summer ever.

" . . . a pictograph of an archer on horseback . . ."

Archer? The overheard word pulled Paley out of her sulk. The Bridles were leaning over a section of the newspaper. "It says they jackhammered out the entire panel," said Mr. Bridle.

"That's such a shame." Ma Etty shook her head. "Why would anyone do that?"

"Same reason people are stealing those fossils. Big money."

Now Sundee perked up. "What did you say about fossils?"

Mr. Bridle handed over the section of the paper. "People have been stealing Native American artifacts and fossils from this area."

"But that's a violation of the Antiquities Act," said Sundee, with a shocked look on her face.

Paley and Leila stared at her like she was speaking Ancient Greek.

"Who cares about a bunch of old rocks?" asked Bryce.

Sundee's eyes looked like they were going to spin out of her head. "Who cares? Who cares?! Patterns of evolution! Ancient climates! Predicting future mass extinctions! Does no one care about science anymore?"

The room was quiet.

Leila stifled a giggle. The Bridles exchanged an amused look.

Cameron put his book down and moved to sit by Sundee. He scanned the newspaper article, then looked up at her and smiled. "I do," he said. "I care about science."

Sundee beamed at him. Bryce started to say something, but Madison quelled him with a look. Paley watched Cameron and Sundee sitting together on the couch, already friends, as if connecting with new people was the easiest thing in the world.

Paley couldn't even connect with a horse.

CHAPTER FIVE

The next morning was Paley's first real horse lesson. All night she had dreamed of racing through the Greensward, and she woke a little more hopeful. Maybe she could win Prince over. She'd been terrible when she started playing *Dragonfyre*, but she'd gotten better. A lot better. Maybe Prince could be her steed if she worked really hard.

Madison had said that's what lessons were for, so Paley scarfed down her breakfast and was the first one out to the barn. When she entered, all the horses poked their noses over their stall doors and huffed at her, but Paley only had eyes for Prince. He stood at attention, his ears pricked forward, and watched her approach.

"Good morning, Your Majesty."

The huge black horse nodded as if saying, *Yes, yes. I know I'm gorgeous.*

Her heart raced the way it did when the Blue Elf was on a quest. Beginnings were exciting. She put her hand up to his nose and stroked him. Everything inside her felt melty like chocolate.

Fletch found Paley like that, running her fingers along Prince's silky nose and dreaming. The trainer came up beside her and rested a hand on the side of Prince's neck. "This is a special horse," he said in his quiet way.

"Special how?" Paley asked.

"Prince doesn't do anything he doesn't believe in. Some horses can be forced to behave. You can bend them to your will. Not Prince. If he connects with you, he'll follow you through storms and worse. You'd be amazed by the things he's done for Mr. Bridle."

"Like what?"

"Got him out of a wildfire, for one thing."

"Wow," said Paley. "I thought horses were afraid of fire."

Fletch scratched between Prince's ears. "They are."

"What else?" Paley stood on her toes to try the ear scratch.

"One of these days you should ask Mr. Bridle about the time he got Prince to carry a tranquilized black bear."

Paley shivered. "Are there bears around here?"

Fletch chuckled. "Not any you need to worry about. Now let's get back to your horse."

Knowing that Prince had carried a real live bear on his back made Paley even more nervous than she was before. "Um . . . Fletch?"

"Yeah?"

"How am I supposed to make Prince believe in me?"

Fletch smiled at her. "Bring your best self. That's how we connect with each other. Horse or human. And be tough. That helps too."

Paley dropped her hand and stepped back from the stall. "That's impossible."

If she'd said that at home, her mom's face would have gone droopy, but Fletch kept smiling, sad eyes and all. "You're up to it," he said.

Before she could argue with him, the barn door opened and the noise level rose. Prince turned his nose up at the hubbub of the other kids. Fletch pointed to the halter hanging on a hook by the side of Prince's stall. "You know what to do. Just like yesterday. Remember that Prince likes to know the plan in advance."

Paley took the halter. Red was the perfect color for Prince, so regal against his black coat. She breathed in and out, hoping her breath said, *Beautiful*, wishing she had a red velvet cape to wear so they would match. She held the halter under Prince's nose. "This is for you. You'll be so handsome."

He snuffled at the halter. His breath tickled her hand. She hoped he was saying, *For you, princess, anything.*

Fletch helped Paley slide the halter over Prince's ears and buckle it in the right place. He handed Paley the lead rope and opened the stall door for her. When she got close to Prince, Paley thought her heart might burst out of her chest. "Hear ye, hear ye, Prince of All Horses, I am going to hook this to your halter and escort you outside."

He tipped his head closer to Paley and waited while she did so. When she clicked her tongue to ask him to move forward, he strode beside her.

"You're doing great," said Fletch, leading the way into the outdoor arena behind the barn. "I like that confidence. Keep it up."

Paley's stomach flip-flopped. She'd felt confident

the day she'd shown up for the gaming club at her new school. And that hadn't gone well.

Not at all.

"Hang tight a minute," said Fletch. "I'm going to help Madison get everyone else out here."

Alone in the arena, Paley's confidence faltered. Was she supposed to tie Prince up or something? He pranced down the fence trying to get to a big clump of green grass at the next post. She tried to tug him back, but instead he pulled her along with him. She stood next to him while he ate, shifting her weight from one foot to the other.

The other kids were leading their horses into the arena. At the sound of hooves and jingling harnesses, Prince extricated his head from between the fence rails. He gave the others a particularly haughty look before dipping his head to snuffle her shoulder. His breath tickled her neck. He poked his nose at her pockets.

That meant he liked her, right? Maybe this would turn out okay.

"Dude," said Madison, coming up beside them and pushing Prince's nose away from Paley, "are you being a pain?"

He snorted.

"Don't let him do that. That's a personal space problem."

"I . . . uh . . ." Paley stammered. "I thought that meant we were getting to know each other."

"It means he hopes you have treats in that pocket of yours. He's being naughty."

Paley's chin dropped to her chest.

"Okay, everyone." Madison clapped her hands to get their attention. "Our lesson today is about personal space. It's important with horses—and boyfriends," Madison added with an over-the-top wink.

Fletch groaned at her joke. Leila laughed out loud.

"Sundee is going to show all of you how to maintain personal space." Madison gestured to Sundee, who was standing next to a butter-colored mare. "Face your horse. Step close, and then ask your horse to step backward by flicking the lead rope side to side."

Sundee nodded and gave the lead rope attached to her horse's halter a quick shake. The metal clasp on the halter rattled, and immediately the horse took a step backward. She stood watching Sundee with her ears pricked forward.

"Excellent," Madison said. "She's paying close attention to you."

Sundee beamed like a fairy-tale princess.

"I want everyone to spread out and practice," said Madison.

Across the arena, Leila had her pony walking backward like it was the easiest thing in the world. Madison headed over to Bryce and Cameron, who were arguing about something.

Paley turned to Prince. "Okay, Your Majesty. We're going to walk back." She tried to sound confident, but her stomach was full of jitters. Why would this horse listen to her? The only thing she knew anything about was a make-believe game, which, as her dad was always pointing out, *did no one any good.*

"Ready?" she asked, looking dubiously at the rope in her hands.

Prince's ears poked forward at her.

She shook the lead rope. It swung back and forth like a limp jump rope.

Prince stared at her but didn't move.

"Face him and hold the lead rope so there's plenty of slack," said Fletch, ambling up beside her. "More flick of the wrist."

Paley tried again. The red rope wobbled through the air. Prince looked both bored and big. She had to crick her neck up to really look at him. Why would he do anything for a pipsqueak like her?

"Come on, Paley," Fletch urged. "Don't let him be in charge."

Sweat trickled down her neck. "I can't," she stammered. Prince swung his head around to scratch an itchy spot on his back, jerking the lead rope through her hands.

"You need to be the boss."

Paley wanted to drop the rope and run. It was just like at her new school. She'd tried to say hello to a few girls. They'd tossed a halfhearted hello her way and gone back to their circle of friends. Why bother trying when they all knew how this was going to end?

"Steady now. It's okay," said Fletch. Paley wasn't sure if he was talking to her or to the horse. "Let's do this together."

Fletch adjusted the rope in Paley's hands so it was the right length and then wrapped his hand around Paley's. Together they gave the rope a quick flick. Prince's ears shot forward. He stared at them.

"He's listening," Fletch whispered. "Tell him to move back in a big strong voice. Not mean. Strong. Then we're going to repeat the message with the rope and a step toward him. Okay?"

Paley nodded. Feeling Fletch towering over her made Paley feel a little better, like she had a regiment of elf warriors guarding her flank. She took a deep lungful of crisp mountain air and said, "Back!"

Together Paley and Fletch flicked the lead. The red rope jumped into action, snaking through the air between her and Prince. He stepped back and stared at her. Fletch stilled the rope, squeezed Paley on the shoulder, and nodded his approval. "Good. Now lead him in a circle around the arena. When you get back here, tell him to stop. If he doesn't stop right away, send him back a few steps."

Paley tightened her grip on the rope and clicked her tongue. "Come on."

Right away she felt resistance. The success she'd felt earlier drained away. Fletch smacked Prince on the rump, and he walked forward, half pulling Paley along. She scrambled to stay on her feet and keep up with him.

"Man, look at her." Bryce's loud voice cut the sound of horses. "Who's walking who?"

Paley's heart sank. She jogged beside Prince until he settled into an easy walk around the arena like that was exactly what he had planned to do all along. Paley forced a smile when she passed Bryce, hoping her expression said, *Yeah, I've got this.*

They were almost back where they started. Prince showed no signs of stopping. A lump rose in Paley's throat. Fletch's pep talk in the barn about making connections and being tough had been short on the practical. How exactly did you stop a giant horse with a mind of his own?

A sick feeling bloomed in the pit of Paley's stomach. She had to get him to stop. Paley took a deep breath, dug her heels in, and said, "Whoa!" Prince pushed past, jerking her after him. "Stop!" she shrieked. Prince took two more steps before he paused and swung his head toward her as if to say, *You talking to me, girly?*

Paley was pretty sure this was not the kind of connection Fletch was talking about.

Suddenly, she was right in front of Bryce. "What's wrong with your horse?" he said, leaning against the fence like he was holding it up.

"Nothing," said Paley, trying to stop panting.

"He seems kinda dumb."

Heat spread up Paley's face. Prince wasn't dumb. It wasn't his fault.

Bryce continued. "My horse does everything I ask the first time. I bet I can make your old gluepot hustle." He pushed off from the fence and snatched

Prince's lead rope from her hands. "Watch and learn, Pay-Lee," he said, turning her name into a taunt.

He strode right up to Prince's nose and shook the rope. "Move!"

Prince remained motionless.

Paley wanted to grab the rope back. She wanted to push Bryce out of the way, but he was huge, a full head taller than her. She froze, like she'd been stunned by some spell, and stayed frozen while Bryce whipped the rope through the air and shouted, "MOVE, YOU DUMB HORSE!"

All sounds in the arena ceased. Prince still didn't budge.

And then like some evil warlock, Bryce raised his arm and slapped her big, beautiful horse across the nose.

Paley's mouth dropped open in a wail. Fletch raced toward them. Bryce raised his fist again, but the bigger, older trainer caught it in one hand and urged Bryce out of the arena.

Prince still hadn't moved.

Neither had Paley.

CHAPTER SIX

Paley wasn't even sure how she got into the bunkhouse. All she knew was that she couldn't stop crying. Everything was tears and sweat and snot. She was furious and hurt and frustrated and sad and indignant all at the same time. It was too much, this stupid mess of emotions. Paley swiped at her face with a dirty T-shirt and curled up in a ball on her bunk.

The door creaked open.

Through the wash of tears, she saw Leila peeking in, her eyes wide.

"Go away!" Paley cried, unable to stop the gulping sobs rolling out of her.

The door opened a little more. A guttural rasp escaped Paley's throat, but Leila came into the bunkhouse, a very determined look on her face. She shut the door tight behind her. "Bryce is in big trouble," she said, handing Paley a handful of tissues. "Mr. Bridle and Ma Etty are talking to him now."

"I hate him," said Paley.

Leila stamped her foot on the floor. "He's a bully, a big jerk bully."

Paley gulped air and tried to stop crying. It wasn't working.

"You're doing great with Prince," said Leila.

Oh, Prince—just the thought of him made Paley cry harder. "No, I'm not," she sobbed. "He hates me, and I let Bryce hit him, and . . . and . . . I should have done something." Paley buried her face in the pillow.

Leila patted her shoulder and held out more tissues.

Paley blew her nose and wiped her eyes and made another attempt to get herself under control. Leila smiled at her, a tiny encouraging twist of her lips.

Paley sniffled and asked, "Why are you being so nice to me?"

Leila pulled herself up very straight and made a little frowny face. "You're sad."

A little tendril of good feeling twisted through Paley.

"I can help you with Prince," said Leila.

"Can you make him like me?" As the words came out, Paley's throat felt tight and scratchy all over again.

"It doesn't really matter if he likes you," said Leila. "With horses, respect is more important. Prince isn't listening because he thinks you're a pushover. You've got to stand up to him."

"But what if I can't?" Paley was remembering that first week at her new school.

She'd seen the flyer for the gaming club. She'd shown up Thursday after school just like it said and walked into a room full of boys arguing about some zombie apocalypse game. As soon as they saw her, they fell silent, looked her up and down, and went back to zombies as if she wasn't even in the room. *What's she doing here?* a boy asked in a not-so-silent whisper. *The Girl Scouts are down the hall,* said another. Paley didn't even stay five minutes.

Leila shrugged. "I think you can."

"How come you're here?" Paley asked. "You seem so perfect."

"That's a joke." Leila fiddled with the button on the cuff of her riding shirt. "You are looking at Exhibit A: Wanton Destruction of Property."

"Huh?"

Leila sighed and stared at the floor. "I put sugar in the gas tank of my mom's Mercedes." Paley's mouth dropped open. "And in the tanks of the other doctors' cars. The whole clinic, believe it or not. It ruined all of them. Will you still be my friend even if I'm a total felon?"

"Um," Paley stammered. "Yes . . . I guess. Why did you do that?"

"All my mom does is work, work, work, and sign me up for a million activities I don't want to do just so she can keep me out of her hair. I wanted to get her attention."

"Well, I guess you did."

"Yeah. Just enough to get sent away for the summer. Convenient for her. How about you?"

"Apparently I was spending too much time online."

"Like how much?"

Paley winced. "Pretty much every waking moment that I wasn't at school."

"Doing what?"

Paley stood, walked over to the dresser, and held up the *Dragonfyre* book.

"Did you play with friends and stuff?"

Paley frowned. "My parents say online friends don't count."

Leila rolled her eyes.

"I know! Right?" Paley put the book back on the shelf. "Anyway, it's their fault that I'm friend-limited in real life."

"What does that mean?"

"My parents made me move last year," said Paley, shrugging, "and everyone in Denver is a jerk."

Leila waggled one finger at her. "I'm from Denver."

Paley bit her lip. "Sorry."

Leila shrugged, reached for Paley's book, and began flipping through it. After a few moments, she said, "You should give Denver a chance. It's pretty cool."

It was Paley's turn to shrug. "I really liked LA."

"You should take the factory tour at Hammond's Candies. It's amazing."

"Maybe."

Leila looked up. "I'm sorry you had to move."

Paley blew her nose again and snuck a peek out of the bunkhouse window. Ma Etty was walking Prince into the barn. He was so beautiful that it made her heart ache. She wanted to race across the fields on his back. She wanted him to leap to her call.

With a horse like that it wouldn't matter that she hadn't made friends in Denver.

Prince would be enough.

\\\

At the end of lunch, Ma Etty took Paley outside on the porch to explain a few things. Bryce glared at her as she left, stabbing his last tortellini with extra force.

"We don't have a lot of rules here," said Ma Etty, gesturing for Paley to sit on the porch steps. "We know you're all good kids."

"Except Bryce," Paley muttered.

Ma Etty patted her knee. "Even Bryce."

Paley was about to protest, but the look Ma Etty gave her made Paley choke back her snarky comment.

"I've seen a lot of kids come through here, and Mr. Bridle and I raised three of our own. There are no bad kids."

Paley picked at a loose sliver of wood on the porch. "Maybe you should tell that to my parents."

Ma Etty didn't rise to the bait. Instead, she said, "The only real rule we have here is respect— respect for the animals, respect for each other, and respect for ourselves. And that's why you and Bryce are sharing the consequences for what happened this morning."

Paley shot off the steps and whirled to face Ma Etty. "You have got to be kidding!" Ma Etty gazed at her placidly. "He hit my horse!" Paley shrieked.

"Prince is your responsibility this summer," said Ma Etty, in the same level tone. "And you allowed Bryce to hurt him. You and Bryce will clean the chicken coop."

"Fine," Paley snapped. "If you want to lump me in with a bully like him, go ahead."

"You are the one who will define your place at this ranch," said Ma Etty. "Hot Tamale and the rest of the ladies will appreciate your help with the housecleaning."

Ten minutes later, Paley and Bryce were outfitted with shovels, rakes, and muck buckets.

"After you shovel out all the old bedding," said Ma Etty, "dump it in the compost heap by the garden and then put down fresh straw. I'll be on the porch if you have any questions."

Paley fumed while she shoveled poop and made faces at the back of Bryce's head. The boy's blond hair was shaved so short near the nape that she could see skin. Paley drew an imaginary dotted line across his neck and drew her imaginary sword. "Thwack," she whispered to the nearest chicken, a shiny red one named Apple Pie.

"What?" said Bryce, leaning on the handle of his pitchfork.

"Nothing." Paley shoveled a pile of filthy straw into the wheelbarrow. The ammonia smell of all the droppings stung her nose.

"Oh, come on. Don't be all mopey."

She attacked another pile. "I'm not mopey."

Bryce slumped in an exaggerated pose of depression. "I'm not mopey," he mocked.

She squeezed the handle of her shovel and kept scooping. The sooner she finished this gross job, the sooner she could get away from stupid old Bryce. A chicken waddled through her work zone, and Paley nudged it away with her foot. Ma Etty was freaking crazy for chickens. They were everywhere!

Bryce picked idly at a pile of straw.

"Could you work, please?" Paley said. "I'd like to get this over with."

"Touchy, touchy."

Paley slammed the shovel into the ground. Three chickens flew up, flapping their wings and squawking in alarm. "I'm not mopey or touchy. I'm mad at you!"

Bryce squinted at her like she was a squeaky rabbit or some small furry thing not worth his time. "Oh, yeah?"

"You hit my horse!"

He made a face at her. "I was trying to get him to behave."

"There are better ways to do that."

"Like what? Mutter at him behind his back? He wasn't exactly following your commands."

"That doesn't make it okay for you to hit him!"

Bryce slammed his right fist into the palm of his other hand. "The only thing anyone listens to is this."

Paley stopped working and stared at him. "Are you from the Stone Age or something?" Sure, she had been imagining his head rolling off his neck and into the dirty straw, but seriously, did Bryce really think he could punch his way out of everything?

He shrugged. "Works for me."

She squinted at him. "Works how?"

Bryce didn't answer. Instead, he made an ugly face and turned his back on her.

Paley shook her head and went back to shoveling,

but she couldn't quell the uncomfortable feeling that filled her. Bryce wasn't doing any better in the friend department than she was. What if they weren't as different as she wanted to believe?

CHAPTER SEVEN

"Rise and shine, cowpokes!" said Madison, flipping on the lights in the bunkhouse. "It is the very best time of the day."

Leila pulled a pillow over her head and groaned.

Sundee sat up in bed, her dark hair in a serious snarl on one side. "How can you say that?"

"One word," said Madison, holding up a finger. "Horses!"

Horses—

Now Paley was the one groaning. Madison's one word brought everything back. Prince's velvety soft nose. The way trading a summer playing *Dragonfyre* for a summer riding Prince seemed okay. Until it wasn't. Until the golden thread broke. Until

Bryce hit him. Until she failed to help.

No more riding lessons for her.

Paley rolled away from the light.

"Come on," said Madison, tugging on her blanket. "It's a new day."

Paley pulled the blanket more tightly around her shoulders. "I'm not getting up."

"Breakfast is in thirty minutes and riding lessons start right after that."

"I'm not riding."

Paley's bed squeaked as Madison sat down beside her. "Prince is waiting for you," she cajoled.

"He doesn't want anything to do with me."

"You've only had one lesson," said Madison. "Do you really think you should be an expert already?"

Through a crack in the blankets, Paley could see Leila tucking her blouse into her jodhpurs. Sundee tamed her hair and pulled on her riding boots. Already experts. "Just leave me alone," she begged.

"Paley—" Madison began, her voice tense, but then she stopped and took a deep breath. "You let me know if you change your mind."

Paley didn't.

As soon as she was alone, Paley brushed her teeth, made her bed, and got dressed. Leaving the lights off, she sat in the dim light of the bunkhouse and looked at her *Dragonfyre* book.

An hour later, the door creaked open. The bright sunlight streaming in made Paley squint. Ma Etty stood framed in the doorway, her silhouette small but fierce all at the same time. Paley bit her lip. It would be just like at home with her parents pleading for her to leave her room, pleading with her to get some fresh air, eat something, *blah blah blah . . .*

But Ma Etty didn't say anything.

She left the door open. She opened the blinds. She flipped on the lights.

She sat down across from Paley. "Look out the window."

Paley looked before she could stop herself. It was like Ma Etty had cast a Compulsion Spell. Prince was in the small warm-up pen, pacing.

Back and forth. Back and forth. The sun shone on his sleek coat, but he wasn't happy. Any idiot could see that. He tossed his head toward the barn, flipped around, stomped to the other side of the pen, flipped his head again.

"What's wrong with him?" she asked, even though she'd meant to give Ma Etty the silent treatment.

"He's cooped up and needs exercise."

Paley bit her lip. "Fletch should take care of him."

"Fletch takes care of Sawbones."

Paley hunched over, feeling more like a cave troll than ever. "He's Mr. Bridle's backup horse."

"He is your responsibility for the summer." That was the dumbest thing Paley had ever heard. Who put a kid like her in charge of a horse like that? "Mr. Bridle and I are confident," Ma Etty continued in a gentle voice, "that you will do the right thing. Why don't you give him a flake of alfalfa and think about it? I'll have Madison meet you out there."

With that, the old lady got up and left Paley alone.

Paley tried not to look out the window, but she couldn't help it. Every time she peeked, Prince was more and more agitated. A horse like that shouldn't be crammed in a tiny pen. He should be racing over the hills. The muscles in his neck rippled under his sleek black coat. She couldn't imagine a more regal horse. Even after yesterday, she wanted to ride him.

She wanted to know what that felt like.

"Fine," she muttered, "just the alfalfa." Paley made her way to the barn, hoping that no one else would see her. The last thing she needed was Bryce making fun of her. But the barn was empty except for the birds in the rafters.

As soon as she appeared with the dried alfalfa, Prince stopped pacing. He snuffled at her and poked his nose over the side of the warm-up pen. His breath tickled her hand, surrounding Paley with the smell of dried apples, oatmeal, and horse sweat. "I brought you a snack," she said, putting the alfalfa next to him.

Paley watched Prince eat. When he was done, he nibbled her braid.

"Hey! That tickles!" She couldn't help giggling.

Prince snuffled at her again.

On the far side of the barn, Paley heard the others. They were laughing. There was Fletch's low murmur, and Madison's cheery encouragement. Those sounds were easy and smooth. Why was it so easy for some people to make friends?

Prince gazed at her with his huge, dark eyes. It was like he was asking, *How hard did you try? How many times?* She kicked the fence post and protested. "I tried!" He stared her down. It was no good. Prince didn't believe her for an instant.

\\\

Ma Etty found her next to the warm-up pen, feeding Prince handfuls of grass. The old woman stood next to Paley, scratched Prince between his ears, and hummed like there was no place else she needed to be. Paley didn't know how to ask Ma Etty what she needed to ask her.

"Um," Paley began. Ma Etty turned toward her, and Paley got tongue-tied.

"What is it, honey?" the old woman asked.

"I think you made a mistake," Paley blurted.

"I'm quite sure I've made plenty. Which particular mess-up are you referring to?"

"Well, it's about Prince," Paley stammered. "Shouldn't I start with a pony or something?"

"Don't you like Prince?"

The horse tilted his head almost as if he understood and was prepared to be insulted.

"Of course I like him! He's incredible."

Prince stretched his neck and shook his mane. *Of course, I am,* he seemed to say

Ma Etty grinned. "Sounds like a match made in heaven."

"But I think I need an easier horse. Prince is too . . ." Paley's words trailed off. The Blue Elf could ride that spectacular horse, but not her.

Ma Etty squeezed her shoulders. "Mr. Bridle and I don't make these decisions lightly. Prince is the right horse for you. Give him a chance. Now, hang tight here. I'm going to tell Madison that you're ready."

And just like that she was gone, leaving Paley protesting to empty air.

"Give him a chance?" She paced back and forth in front of the pen. "Shouldn't he be giving me a chance?" She glared at Prince. "Shouldn't you?"

CHAPTER EIGHT

Noises on the ranch house porch got Paley's attention. Mr. Bridle and Paul were leaving, deep in conversation. The porch door slammed shut behind them, and suddenly all Paley could think about was the office. The computer. The Internet. It drew her like a magnet. It would be so easy . . .

The sound of boots on gravel brought her right back to the warm-up pen.

"Hey there!" said Madison, ridiculously cheerful. "I hope you're ready. I've got something special planned."

Paley frowned. Madison's special something sounded like trouble. "What is it?"

Madison let herself into the warm-up pen

with Prince. "Not punishment, if that's what you're expecting."

"That's what happened yesterday."

"Eh—" said Madison, waving away Paley's gloom and doom. "As Ma Etty always says, *New day, new start*."

Paley thought that she'd heard enough of Ma Etty's famous mottos for one summer. "He doesn't like me." She'd said it before, but this time it seemed true, and Paley felt the prickle of tears behind her eyelids.

"Hey," said Madison, in a softer voice. "Are you okay?"

Paley nodded way too fast, like a bobblehead.

"It was hard when I first came here, too," Madison said.

"You came here?" Paley asked. Madison looked like she belonged on this ranch. Watching her on horseback was like watching a mermaid in the ocean. What kind of troubles could she have had?

"Sure did. When I was twelve, like you. And when I was thirteen. Hard case, you know. It took two years to straighten me out." She laughed like Paley was in on a private joke. "But don't worry. We'll tell this bratty boy who's boss." Madison made a frowny face at Prince, who snuffled in surprise, and Paley couldn't help laughing too.

"Come on." Madison waved her inside the warm-up pen. "You can give him some treats." Madison handed three horse biscuits to Paley and explained how to hold them with her palm flat.

Paley approached Prince feeling like she was about to offer a squashed peanut butter and jelly sandwich to a king, but he picked them off of her hand with his lips like they were delicacies.

"Come on, handsome," Madison said, opening the stall and clipping the red lead rope under Prince's chin. "Since Prince likes to show off," she said to Paley, "we'll go down by the stream instead of into the arena. No audience for Mr. Big Pants."

Prince snorted and swished his tail exactly like he understood what Madison was saying.

Paley walked beside Madison as she led him out of the warm-up pen. Prince was crazy-gorgeous with the sun shining on his coat. She wanted to thunder into battle on his back. Instead, they walked away from the warm-up pen and toward a lopsided butte in the distance. The green fields seemed to go on forever. Sunshine twinkled on the surface of the creek. Even Paley had to admit the ranch was beautiful.

In a big open pasture, Madison asked Prince to stop, which he did without protest. Paley stroked Prince's neck and the regal slope of his nose. She closed her eyes. The breeze touched her cheek, the sun warmed her shoulders, and the horse's nose was the softest thing she'd ever felt.

"You ready?" Madison asked.

Paley's eyes flicked open. "Ready for what?"

"Ready to be in charge of this bad boy."

"No. Yes. I don't know."

Madison grinned at her. "Sounds about right. Now listen up. You talk to him with your body more than anything, okay? You're the one who decides when to go, where to go, and when to stop. Stand firm next to him. Square shoulders. Strong back. Look where you want to go."

Madison demonstrated, and immediately Prince perked up his ears. "See how he's listening?" She made a clicking sound with her tongue and strode forward. Prince walked right along next to her. After ten paces, she said, "Whoa," and he stopped with his nose at her shoulder, ready for her next command.

Madison handed Paley the lead rope. "You try."

Paley took a deep breath and grasped the lead.

Prince's eye rolled toward Madison, who glared at him until he looked straight ahead.

"Tell him hello and ask him to get ready."

Paley stroked his neck. "Hello, Your Majesty. Ready to walk?"

He huffed at her. Paley squared her shoulders, looked straight ahead, and clicked her tongue. He didn't move. Not an inch. Not a muscle. Nothing. She turned toward him and pulled harder. He still didn't budge. "Please come on," she whispered. He pressed one ear back and gave her the stink-eye. A limp, sick feeling slithered down her spine, and she glanced at Madison.

"It's okay," she said. "Try again. Be confident."

Paley tensed her muscles and leaned into the rope. Then she clicked her tongue as hard as she could, praying he would walk for her. Instead, Prince gave his head a shake and jerked the lead rope out of her hand. Paley felt like a fly he'd just swished away with his tail.

"Keep a hold of him," said Madison.

Paley snatched at the rope, feeling her face turn red. "I'm sorry," she stammered.

"You have to be the boss."

"I can't!"

Prince pulled on the rope until he had enough slack to bite off a huge mouthful of grass. He munched, staring at Paley in an I'm–in–charge–here kind of way. Paley's face burned as much as the palm of her hand.

Before Prince could take another bite of grass, Madison took a hold of his halter and pulled his head up. She pointed down the stream. "Look at that cottonwood down there, Paley. That's where I want you to take him."

That was all well and good, but Paley couldn't imagine how to make it happen.

"Here's what you're going to do," Madison continued. "Take the lead rope right under his chin. Hold it tight. Now close your eyes. I want you to imagine you've got a crown on your head. He might be the prince, but you're the queen. Everyone has to obey you."

Paley was dubious. "I don't know how to do that."

"Sure you do," said Madison. "I saw that *Dragonfyre* book. There are some seriously tough warrior-queens in there." Madison put a hand on her shoulder. "Trust me, okay? Close your eyes. Think warrior. Think queen."

Paley squeezed her eyes shut. What if a heavy,

golden crown with a big ruby in the middle rested on the top of her head? She stretched her neck. That's how queens stand: tall and proud. She could picture the Blue Elf triumphant after she defeated the goblin army. She could feel the strength in her sword arm.

"That's right," Madison whispered. "You're Prince's queen. He'll fight for you. He'll carry you like the wind. He'll do anything you ask."

Paley sensed Prince beside her, alert and listening.

"Tell him to go, Your Highness," said Madison.

The hot rays of the sun were like a velvet robe upon Paley's shoulders. She opened her eyes, lifted her chin a little higher, clicked with her tongue, and stepped forward.

Prince matched her.

A thrill raced through Paley. She took another step.

So did Prince.

All the way to the cottonwood, they paced side by side. When Paley stopped under the tree, Prince halted and bowed his head. Tiny fluffs of white—the seeds of the tree—fell down on them like fairy blessings.

CHAPTER NINE

Paley floated through lunch, lost in instant replays of the moment when she and Prince had moved through falling cloud fluff like they were connected.

It was magic.

Tomorrow they'd work at the stream again. That's what Madison had promised. Paley was nervous but excited. She craved that feeling of connection when Prince had responded to her.

I made that happen, she thought. *I really did.*

It was better than pretending. It felt real. And it made her feel like she was something bigger than she'd known before.

Mealtime was winding down. Leila and Cameron were getting dish duty directions. Bryce was arguing with Ma Etty about having to weed the garden when Paul interrupted them, clapping his hands to get their attention. "Begging your pardon, Ma Etty," he said, tipping his hat to her. "I need everyone for a high-priority rescue mission."

Paley handed her plate to Leila and turned to listen to Paul.

"As you know—or maybe you don't—Quartz Creek Ranch is a working cattle ranch in spite of the fact that Mr. Bridle is obsessed with baby goats." Mr. Bridle chuckled into his coffee. "And we've got ourselves a situation. One of my cows is missing."

Paley looked around the kitchen. Fletch was trying not to crack up, and Madison nearly spit coffee over the table.

"I'm serious, Madison!" Paul protested.

Now she was laughing in earnest. "Which cow? Which one of your babies is on the lam? Daisy? Pookie-Pie? Sally Lou?"

Fletch couldn't hold it in any longer. He leaned over, slapping his thighs and roaring.

Paul pulled his hat even farther down on his head. "If you must know, it's Lorraine, and I'm worried she might have busted through the fence into the Goodsteins' place."

Madison and Fletch stopped laughing immediately and started pulling on their boots. "What are we waiting for?" asked Fletch. "Lorraine doesn't stand a chance."

"Come on, girls," Madison said, gathering up Paley, Sundee, and Leila. "Let's change out of our riding gear so we can help Paul."

"Afternoon chores are cancelled," said Ma Etty. "I'll finish cleaning up. Get going before Delia Goodstein gets her mitts on Lorraine."

As soon as they were in the girls' bunkhouse, Madison barked orders. "Jeans and decent shoes— hiking boots or sneakers. And sunscreen," she added before going into her room to change.

Sundee went into the shared bathroom. Paley didn't have proper riding clothes, so she just stayed in her jeans and cowboy boots. When Sundee was done, Leila went in.

Madison emerged in dirty jeans, with her hair tied back in a bandana. "Where's Leila?"

"Here," said the girl, coming out of the bathroom looking like an L.L. Bean model. Her shirt still had a tag on it.

Madison eyed Leila's outfit. "Paul's expeditions are notoriously messy."

"I don't have anything scrappier than this. My mom packed for me." Leila scowled at her stiff new jeans. "I'll be fine."

Madison shrugged. "Okay, then. Let's go rescue Lorraine. Poor thing."

Paul was waiting for them out front. He had two off-road vehicles that he called Rangers ready to go. To Paley they looked like golf carts on steroids. Each one had two rows of seats, tires with big, knobby treads, and a roof but no doors. One was blue and the other was green.

The boys came out of their bunkhouse arguing.

"I wouldn't be caught dead reading a book about a girl," Bryce announced.

Cameron flipped his curly hair out of his eyes. "That's just dumb."

"Are you calling me dumb?"

Cameron stepped aside as Bryce pushed into his space. "No, I'm not calling you dumb, but it's a good book. You should read it."

Bryce snorted and was about to go on harassing Cameron when Paul called him over to learn how to check the oil in the blue Ranger.

"Man," said Cameron, wiping his forehead with the back of his hand and letting out a big breath, "that guy."

"What are you reading?" asked Paley.

"*A Ring of Archers.*"

"I loved that book!"

A wide smile exploded across his face. "I know. I've read it, like, ten times. It's my favorite. After the first time, I asked my mom to let me take archery." His face fell. "Of course, she said no, but one of these days I'm going to learn to shoot a bow."

"That would be cool," said Paley. "You can play an archer in *Dragonfyre* if you earn—"

"Hey, folks," said Paul, interrupting all conversations, "we've got to find Lorraine."

"Madison," said Paul, tossing her a set of keys, "take the green Ranger and the girls and ride north along the fence between us and the Goodsteins'. We'll start at the butte and drive south toward you."

Madison caught the keys and nodded. "Meet you in the middle!"

"Got your phone?" Paul asked.

She pulled it out of her pocket like she was a fast-draw target shooter. "Always ready!"

"Hey!" Bryce protested. "What about the no-cell-phone rule?"

Paul grinned at him. "Ranch business. Come on, boys. You're with me."

"Shotgun!" yelled Bryce, elbowing Cameron out of the way and plopping down next to Paul in the front seat of the other Ranger. Cameron frowned but didn't say a word as he climbed in back.

"That was mean," muttered Paley.

Leila snorted. "Bryce is a bully."

"All right, girls," said Madison, shooing them into the vehicle. "Ma Etty says no trash talk."

"But he totally pushed Cameron out of the way," said Paley, hanging back so Leila could take the front seat, and then climbing in back with Sundee.

"Yup." Madison revved the engine. "Cameron will have to learn to stand up for himself."

"That's it?" Paley couldn't believe it.

"Bryce should be nicer," said Sundee.

"Yup," Madison repeated.

"Aren't you guys supposed to fix us or something?" Leila said, disgusted.

Madison laughed as she turned the Ranger toward the fence line that separated the ranch from the Goodsteins' place to the east. "My job is to teach you to ride. As Ma Etty says, *Being a good human is up to you.*"

"What's with all the Ma Etty quotes?" asked Sundee as they bounced along.

Madison swerved around a big pothole in the dirt track.

"When you've been around here long enough, you'll know 'em too."

\\

Fifteen minutes later, the track they were on turned north and ran parallel to the fence. On the other side was a rolling field of wheat in neat rows and another dirt track, paralleling their own. Paley could see a farmhouse in the distance. Nobody talked anymore. It was too hot and dry for that. Paley squinted against the sun and held on. Twenty minutes later, they caught sight of a vehicle in the distance far ahead of them. It kicked up billowing clouds of dust.

"I hope that's not the Goodsteins," said Madison, cutting the engine of the Ranger.

"Maybe it's the guys," Sundee suggested.

Madison shaded her eyes with her hands and squinted. "I don't think so."

Seeing Madison so serious when she almost always had a grin on her face sent a shiver down Paley's spine.

"Why is everyone so freaked out about the Goodsteins?" Leila asked.

"I shouldn't have said anything," Madison sighed. "Neighborly love and all that."

"But—" Leila prompted.

"They are the worst neighbors ever," Madison continued. "Not big fans of what we do here. Always harping on Ma Etty and Mr. Bridle to keep their animals—and by that they mean all of us—off their land. Anything goes wrong at the Goodsteins' place, and they find a way to blame us." She put the Ranger back in drive with a grim expression.

The dirt track was so bumpy that Paley's teeth kept knocking together, and her braid was flopping everywhere.

"Watch the fence line," said Madison. "Remember, we're looking for breaks. If Lorraine is in their wheat fields, I don't know what we'll do."

On the Bridles' side of the fence, acres and acres of pasture spread out across rolling hills. Here and there Paley saw a cluster of cows grazing placidly. The wild jolts of the careening Ranger seemed of little interest to them. On the Goodsteins' side, the land sloped gradually down and away.

"Crap," said Madison, gritting her teeth. "Don't mention Lorraine, okay?"

Paley looked up to see the vehicle, a battered Jeep with jacked-up wheels, parked ahead of them on the opposite side of the fence. "Should we turn back?" she asked.

"We're not doing anything wrong," said Sundee.

Madison slowed the Ranger down. "Let me do the talking."

On the other side of the barbed-wire fence, three teenagers lounged on the hood of the mud-splattered Jeep. A lanky, pale boy with slicked-back brown hair sneered at them. "I see you've got a new crop of losers." The other boys laughed.

Madison glowered at him. "Go back to Grandma, Thomas. We're on a tour of the ranch. Good clean fun. Unlike you guys."

"Who, me?" Thomas held up his hands and made a face like he couldn't believe the accusations. "We're out collecting. Good clean fun."

She pursed her lips. "Right. I believe that."

Thomas flashed an oily smile. As Madison brought the Ranger back up to speed, he called after her. "I hope the parade goes better for you this year!"

"Who was that?" asked Paley.

Madison wiped a hand across her brow. "That's the Goodsteins' grandson and his dumb gang, the Rock Hounds."

"Are they into geology?" Sundee asked.

"Supposedly. They sell rocks and minerals to the shop in town, I think, but they seem to be more interested in causing trouble."

Leila leaned forward. "What did he mean about the parade?"

"Every year, we ride in the Fourth of July parade," Madison explained. "Last year, they set off a cherry bomb right behind my horse, Snow White. She bolted down Main Street right before the parade kicked off. I missed the whole thing."

CHAPTER TEN

Madison and the girls continued driving along the barbed-wire fence. So far, so good. There was no sign that Lorraine had broken through.

"She's probably sleeping in the shade somewhere," Sundee said. "I want to go back. It's too hot."

Leila nodded her agreement. "I was hoping we could do the soccer thing with Cupcake."

Madison shook her head. "We've got to keep going until we meet the guys."

Up ahead, the terrain was getting rocky, and the fence went up and down with the contours of the land. The track was getting worse.

"Is that Fool's Butte?" Sundee asked, pointing to the huge rock formation up ahead.

Madison nodded.

"How did you know that?" Leila asked Sundee, bracing herself against the bumps.

"I was checking out a map of the ranch. There's supposed to be an old mine in it."

"A gold mine?" Paley asked, already imagining a dragon's treasure.

"That's what the pioneers thought when they came to Quartz Creek," said Madison.

"I get it," Leila crowed. "They were thinking megabucks and it turned out to be worthless. And then to have it named after you—Fool's Butte—ouch!"

Madison stopped the Ranger at a spot where the track seemed to vanish in the jumble of boulders. "We've got to split up here," she said, getting out. "Look."

The four of them were standing on the edge of a steep, rocky slope that dropped away to the right. The fence disappeared over the edge and was swallowed by a thicket of bushes and small trees at the base of the drop-off. Paley could see where it emerged in the distance on the other side of the ravine. Down below, where the ground flattened out again, there was a low, marshy area. Then it became the Goodsteins' wheat field, stretching as far as Paley could see.

"I have to drive the Ranger around this steep bit," said Madison, pointing to the left where Paley could see faint wheel tracks taking a wide circle around the rocky area. "But Lorraine might have muddled her way down the ravine. There's a spring down there that the cows sometimes like to drink at. Follow the fence line on foot. I'll meet you on the other side. Holler if you see Lorraine."

"Are you sure that's safe?" asked Sundee.

Leila rolled her eyes and grabbed Paley's hand. "Let's go."

"Whatever you do," said Madison, "don't cross the fence onto their property." The noise of the Ranger faded as they dropped over the edge.

"I don't like this," Sundee whined as they clambered down the steepest part of the rock fall.

Paley and Leila exchanged annoyed looks.

"At least it's cooler in here," Paley offered, but Sundee kept whining about the sharp rocks and the possibility of rattlesnakes and who lets kids go chasing after cows anyway.

Paley pushed through the thick shrubs and peered this way and that for Lorraine. The ground was getting softer. Paley figured she must be getting close to the spring. A few feet farther on, she stepped over a deep, hoof-shaped depression that was filled with water. Then another, and another.

"Hey! Over here!" she called.

Leila crashed through the brush toward her. "Awesome!" she said, grinning wildly when Paley pointed at the tracks. "Looks like cow to me!"

Sundee caught up with them, panting and red-faced. "Did you find her?"

"Practically!" said Leila.

"Good," said Sundee. "Let's go find Madison and get out of here."

The other girls stared at her. "No way," said Leila.

"Yeah," said Paley, "we've got to follow the tracks."

"Through the fence?" Sundee said, pointing past them. Sure enough, a small tree had fallen, taking down a section of fence, and the tracks were headed straight for the Goodsteins'.

"We can't let them get Lorraine!" Paley protested.

Sundee put her hands on her hips. "We'll get in trouble."

Leila threw up her hands. "We're already in trouble. That's why we're at the ranch."

Sundee looked like she'd swallowed a toad.

"Come on," Leila said to Paley. "Let's get Lorraine."

Paley looked from one mad face to the other,

shrugged at Sundee, and followed Leila through the fence. After a minute, Paley could hear Sundee following them. The ground grew even softer. Their boots made a squelching sound with every step. Paley's pants were splattered with mud. Her senses were on high alert, looking for Lorraine and listening for the sound of Thomas Goodstein's truck.

Just when she thought maybe they should turn back, Paley caught a flash of black and white behind a clump of bushes. There was Lorraine, knee-deep in mud. The cow pulled up a big mouthful of new wheat, gazed at the girls with liquid brown eyes, and chewed.

"We've got to go, you guys," Sundee pleaded. "The Bridles are going to kick us off the ranch."

Paley frowned at her. "Not without Lorraine. No one gets left behind!"

"She's huge," said Sundee. "How are you going to get her to come? She's not a dog."

"I don't know. Let me think." Paley wracked her brain. If only she could cast a Summoning Spell, but this was real life. Faint engine noise became audible over the birdsong and the sound of Lorraine chewing. She had to think of something.

"My belt!"

Leila beamed. "Yes!"

"This is nuts," said Sundee.

"Well, go back to Madison, then," Leila snapped. "We're saving Lorraine!"

Paley didn't bother to watch Sundee stomp off toward where they were supposed to meet Madison. Instead she unbuckled her belt and looped it around Lorraine's neck. The cow chewed and stared and chewed some more.

Leila crooned at Lorraine. "It's okay, honey. We're going to save you from those nasty neighbors."

"Come on," Paley urged, giving the belt a tug.

Nothing.

She pulled harder and looked at Leila. "What do we do?"

Leila sucked on her lower lip, thinking hard, then she snapped her fingers. "Got it!" Leila wrenched up several large handfuls of wheat and held them in front of Lorraine's nose. The cow nibbled. Leila backed up. "Keep coming, Lorraine. Tasty nibbles right here." Together the two girls urged the cow toward the Bridles' property. Leila kept offering food. Paley kept tugging. Every step sent mud flying. Paley could feel it splattering her face and arms, and she couldn't stop smiling. Paley wanted to cheer out loud.

Until they reached Sundee and caught sight of Madison.

"What in the—?" Madison slammed her hands on her hips. "Girls!"

Paley's victorious feeling sank right down into her soaked boots.

"Look," said Leila, with guilt-tinged cheeriness. "We found her."

Madison's face was pinched. "You are on the Goodsteins' property."

"But . . ." Paley began.

Madison glared harder.

"I told them not to go," Sundee squeaked. Leila shot dagger eyes at her. Lorraine mooed and nudged Leila's hand for another mouthful of wheat.

Paley heard the rumble of a motor. "Is that them?" she asked, panic rising.

"You'd better hope not," huffed Madison. "Let's go." She got behind Lorraine and smacked her on the rump. "Pull!"

With Madison in the back helping, they managed to get Lorraine moving. Once they were safely on the Bridles' land, Paley risked a look at Leila. Her brand-new shirt was a mess and her hair was full of twigs from climbing through the thicket.

Leila's freckles were obscured under a splatter of mud. Paley couldn't help it. She started to giggle. "You're filthy!"

A snort escaped Leila—a very unladylike snort. "So are you!"

Paley tried to smother her giggles, but every time she looked at Leila, they came back, bigger than before. Back at the Ranger, Madison silenced them with a glare. She punched numbers on her cell phone so vigorously that Paley thought she might break it. The conversation with Paul was clipped and brief. "Yes. We have her. Bottom of the ravine. Yes. I know. I'll let the Bridles handle it."

Handle it?

Paley knew what Madison meant. She meant handle *them*.

Still, Paley couldn't stop grinning. No matter what awful chore the Bridles gave her, she and Leila had completed their quest, and Lorraine was safe. It was a victory!

\\\

The zinging, happy feeling didn't last long. As they drove slowly back to the ranch, leading Lorraine, the usually cheerful, chatty Madison was like a little black cloud of death. She only spoke to give commands. *Shorten her rope up. Don't pull on her neck.* Sundee ignored them too, except once when she leaned in and said, "You'd better not get me into trouble."

Back at the ranch, the three girls were banished to their bunkhouse while Madison, Paul, and the Bridles conferred. Leila tried to get a card game going, but no one was interested. Sundee kept peeking out the window to see if anyone was coming. Paley thought it was all a lot of fuss for nothing. She was in the bathroom wiping the mud off her face when she had an idea.

A great idea!

"Hey," she said, going back into the main room. "I know what our cabin name should be— the Mud Rustlers! You know, like cattle rustlers but unwashed."

"That's funny," said Leila. "I like it!"

"It sounds illegal," said Sundee, frowning.

Leila threw up her hands. "Oh my gosh, Sundee. Stop being so perfect. What did you do to get sent here anyway? Get a B on something?"

A wave of emotion flooded Sundee's face. She

spluttered like a teakettle overflowing. "Who told you that?"

"Told me what?" Leila asked, confused. She looked to Paley for an explanation.

Paley shrugged. She was as lost as Leila, but it was pretty clear Sundee was about to cry.

"About the grades!" Sundee wailed.

Leila held out her hands. "Calm down. I was messing with you."

But it was way too late for that. Sundee collapsed on her bunk in tears. Paley bit her lip. Sundee rubbed her the wrong way, but it was awful to see her so upset. She sat down beside her and patted her shoulder.

"What happened?" she asked.

Sundee's words were muffled by her pillow when she said, "I got a B in advanced math."

Paley looked at Leila. It was her turn to shrug. "That's good, isn't it?"

Sundee pushed herself up, indignant. "I have never had a B, not ever!"

Paley thought of her own marginal performance in math. "Okay, then. That sucked, I guess."

"I got sent here," she said, grimacing at Leila, "because I hacked the school computer and changed my grade to an A. But my teacher noticed and had the school look into it, and I got caught."

"Oh," said Leila.

"And I don't want to talk about it again, okay?"

"Okay," said Paley, and Leila added, "Case closed."

CHAPTER ELEVEN

The girls kept their promise, and when the Bridles came to talk to them, they explained that Sundee had tried to stop them from going onto the Goodsteins' property. Sundee flashed them a grateful smile, but Paley and Leila didn't get off the hook so easily.

The next day after lessons, Madison and Fletch took Sundee and Cameron into town for ice cream. Paley sighed as she watched them drive down Bridlemile Road. "I want cookies-and-cream."

"I know," said Leila. "They're going to register for the Fourth of July parade, too."

"While we've got manure duty," said Paley, staring at three huge piles of horse poop—fresh, medium, and old. Their job was shoveling the old, composted stuff into wheelbarrows and spreading it in the garden. And joy, oh, joy, they got Bryce on top of that. The way he'd been pushing Cameron around had not gone unnoticed after all.

Ma Etty had handed out gloves and shovels and rakes, and now she and Mr. Bridle were sitting in the shade of the porch working on the ranch accounting while the girls suffered.

All for rescuing Lorraine! It was so unfair.

Paley jammed her shovel in the pile and hefted another load into the wheelbarrow. It didn't smell as bad as the fresh stuff, but it was still gross. She tried to imagine she was shoveling rubies or diamonds into an iron-bound strongbox.

It didn't work.

After an hour, they stopped for a water break and clustered in the shade of the porch. Bryce was flushed and sweating, Leila was too tired to talk, and the Bridles were deeply engrossed in rows of numbers when Paley heard a truck on the road. The crew cab pickup was so shiny new that road dust practically refused to settle on it. The vehicle pulled to a stop near the house, and two people climbed out. One was a heavyset man in a red plaid shirt and a trucker hat. The other was a squat, slightly bowlegged woman with short-cropped brown hair.

"Willard," the man said.

"Good morning, Jim. Delia," answered Mr. Bridle.

The woman strode toward the porch, her eyes drilling into the Bridles. "We've got a bone to pick with you."

Mr. Bridle took a deep breath. "What's troubling you now, Delia?"

"There is new fencing in the ravine."

"Yup."

"Why'd you redo it?" Her voice grated on Paley.

Mr. Bridle took off his hat and ran his fingers through his short hair, making it stick out crazy. "Well, Delia . . ." he began, speaking slowly and almost managing to keep the irritation out of his voice. "Etty and I are always trying to keep the place nice. Been ranching here a long time. Things wear out."

"If you really wanted to improve our property values," she snapped, "you would stop having them kids around." Delia Goodstein raked across them with her eyes. "I saw the tracks in the mud. Which one of you delinquents done it?"

Paley felt like she'd swallowed concrete. Leila's eyes were bugging out of her head. Bryce set his cup down with a bang. All of them kept their mouths glued shut. No one in their right mind would admit anything to that woman. She might bite your head off.

Mr. Bridle broke the tension by rising from the porch and walking down the steps to meet the Goodsteins. "We've been neighbors for a long time," said Mr. Bridle. "We don't see eye to eye on much. I don't see why I have to keep repeating myself. But here we are. Again. These kids," he said in his steady, calm way, "are not delinquents. They are not trouble. They are not a problem for you or for me or for my lovely wife."

The woman sneered. "Your little angels broke into my—"

Mr. Bridle cut her off. "Several of my guests rescued a cow that had gone astray. She was lucky they came along. I am lucky they came along. And Paul has repaired the fence, so we are finished here."

She put her hands on her hips and turned toward her husband. "Can you believe this? Can you believe him talking to me like that? Look at that one." She pointed at Bryce, who was glaring like he wanted to show her what *delinquent* really meant. "He's a walking mugshot. And you"—she fixed her ugly little eyes on Paley—"I can tell a criminal when I see one."

A hot rush of tears choked Paley. She squeezed her eyes shut to stop them from coming. She'd wanted to help Lorraine, not to cause trouble for the Bridles. Oh why, oh why did her parents send her here? She should be home in her cave doing the only thing she knew how to do.

Delia Goodstein stomped down the stairs toward the pickup, sweeping her husband along behind her. Before she shut the door, she waggled one finger at the kids on the porch and said, "You'd better stay off our land! We'll be watching you, and next time we catch you, you won't get off this easy."

Everyone on the porch stood frozen until the truck roared off.

As soon as they disappeared around a bend in the road, Ma Etty wrapped her arms around Paley. "That woman doesn't know a thing about you. Not one single thing."

Mr. Bridle laid his hand on Bryce's shoulder. "She is very good at jumping to conclusions and very poor at seeing the truth."

"Where's the sugar?" spat Leila. "I'll fix their stupid truck."

"Leila . . ." Ma Etty warned.

"Why don't you three finish up in the garden?" said Mr. Bridle.

As they headed to the wheelbarrows, Paley wiped away tears. Leila's offer of sabotage had helped. A little. A warm starburst feeling in her chest pushed back Delia Goodstein's ugly words. But the tears were not cooperating.

"You'll get used to it," said Bryce.

Paley looked up at him. "Used to what?"

"Used to people assuming the worst about you." He went back to work without another word, slamming each shovelful into the wheelbarrow with such force that it shook. Paley didn't think he was as *used to it* as he wanted her to believe. The red blotches on Bryce's face seemed like more than the heat.

"She is a jerk," said Leila.

"Yup." Bryce looked back to where the Goodsteins had come from. Nothing but road dust was left of the truck. "Are you done blubbing?" he asked Paley. She glared at him. "Good," he said, appraising her. "Mad is better."

"Better than what?" Paley snapped.

"Better than *wah, wah, wah, poor me.*"

Now Paley was steaming. "Did you hear that lady?"

"Next time I see her, do you want me to punch her?"

Leila stopped shoveling. "Wait. What?"

Paley couldn't make sense of what he was saying. Was Bryce trying to be *nice*?

He sighed like she was as dumb as a post. "I said I'll punch her. If you want me to, that is." He ducked his head, suddenly shy, which was the weirdest thing of all. Paley stared at him, gobsmacked. "Since she was mean to you," he continued, still not meeting her eyes.

"Are you . . . um . . . offering to fight for me?" she asked.

Bryce avoided her gaze and went back to shoveling. "Well . . . yeah."

Paley gaped. "Thanks. I think."

Bryce didn't look up. "You're welcome."

"But let's not, okay?"

"Okay. I'm just saying . . . "

Leila held up her hands like she needed to stop the world from turning. "What just happened here? Why are you always talking about beating people up?"

The wheelbarrow was full. With a grunt, Bryce hefted the handles and pushed it toward the garden, and the girls followed with the tools. Paley hoped that Leila hadn't ticked him off, but when she caught a glimpse at his face, he wasn't mad, just serious. "I guess because it works. No one messes with you."

"How do you have any friends if you are threatening people all the time?" Leila asked.

"Who needs friends?"

Paley thought about her new school and her new neighborhood and all the faces of all the kids who wouldn't even give her the time of day. "I do," she said in a small voice.

He shrugged.

"What's it like to hit someone?" Paley asked.

Bryce shrugged again. "Hurts your hand."

Paley picked up the rake and started spreading manure. The wooden handle was rough on her palms. She squeezed hard, noticing the flex of bone and muscle. How would it hurt? Like breaking or bruising or crushing? Would it hurt more than the person who got hit? She had thought Bryce was a bully, a higher-order goblin warrior, armored and nearly invincible, but even he had a soft spot.

"If it hurts, why do you do it?" Leila asked.

Bryce leaned on the rake. For a minute Paley thought he wasn't going to answer, but then he said, "There were these guys in fifth grade who used to pick on me all the time. Pour glue in my desk. Pull my hair. It used to be long," Bryce explained. He spit off to one side, looking disgusted. "All the time in the library—*yank, tug, pull*. I hated them."

"What happened?"

"I got big at the end of sixth grade, I cut my hair really short, and I beat them both up. After that, no one ever bothered me again." He wasn't bragging. Just stating the facts. After a moment, he added, "It always helps for a second, but as soon as you do . . . as soon as you hear the crunch, you wish you could take it back."

"Oh," said Leila, stunned.

"Anyway, after that no one bothered me. Everyone just steered clear."

Of course they did. When Paley thought about Prince and the horrible sound of Bryce's hand on his velvety nose, she wanted to steer clear, too. She had wanted to have the Blue Elf chop off his head. And somehow, knowing that Bryce probably felt bad, even if he wouldn't admit it, made everything worse.

Why couldn't she just go back in her cave? It was easy there. No Bryce. No Goodsteins. No trouble. Paley twitched uncomfortably. If she left Quartz Creek Ranch, she would have to leave Prince. When she had worked with him by the stream, something magical had happened. The real kind. And she wanted more of it.

There was only one thing to do.

Paley took a deep breath. Queens had a certain responsibility to do the hard things. She pulled herself as straight and tall as she could, feeling the weight of a crown on her forehead. "Hey, Bryce," she said, forcing herself to look right at him.

He shoved the rake at a pile of manure. "What?"

"You can't hit my horse again."

He stiffened. She saw his hands flex on the handle of the rake. He stared down his nose at her.

She stared right back, even though her legs went wobbly underneath her. "I know you wish you hadn't done it. So I'm going to let it go this time. But never again. Okay?"

A muscle twitched at his temple. This might be the moment when she found out what it was like to take a punch. Paley fought the urge to run away.

But suddenly, the tension seemed to leave him.

He smiled at her—actually smiled—and said, "Okay. But I'm not making any promises about the Goodsteins."

CHAPTER TWELVE

Paley and Madison worked with Prince down by the stream for a few more days, which was fine by Paley. Getting to know Bryce, Sundee, and Leila was good, but it was also complicated. She was starting to see that everyone had some issues to work on.

At least things were getting better with Prince now that she understood it was her job to make him feel secure.

"As long as you are confident about what you want him to do," Madison reminded her, "he'll do anything you ask."

"Like how he went through the fire for Mr. Bridle?" she asked.

"Exactly!" said Madison.

Sometimes Paley didn't know what to do. When that happened, she waited, calming her breath and stroking Prince's neck.

"There's nothing wrong with asking him to wait," said Madison. "You're in charge."

By the end of the week, Madison decided they were ready to ride.

"Are you sure?" Paley asked as they got ready in the barn one morning.

"Ask him," said Madison, walking up to Prince with his saddle on one arm. Immediately the big horse nosed the oiled leather, and the trainer laughed. "I guess that's your answer. Let's tack him up."

"I've already groomed him and picked his hooves," said Paley, hoping she sounded more confident than she felt.

Madison grinned at her. "No kidding! He's so shiny I can practically see my reflection in his coat." Paley's face grew warm, and she stood up tall. It felt good to know how to take care of Prince, and it felt even better to have Madison notice how hard she was trying.

After they had saddled him, Madison showed her how to hold the bridle and how to ask Prince to accept the bit by holding it up to his nose with one hand and wiggling a finger into the side of his mouth.

"Go ahead," said Madison. "Be confident."

"That's easy for you to say," said Paley. "What if he bites my finger off?"

"He doesn't have teeth back there," the trainer explained, and sure enough, when Paley took a deep breath and stuck a finger inside his mouth, the skin was pillow soft and slobbery. Paley slid the bit into place. "Nicely done," said Madison, helping her to get the crown piece up over his ears.

Once all the buckles were buckled, Madison dropped into an exaggerated bow and gestured toward the door to the barn. "After you, Queen Paley."

Paley tipped her head as regally as she could manage and led Prince out of the barn toward the grove of cottonwoods by the stream. All the groundwork they had been doing together was paying off. The big horse didn't balk once.

"I'm going to clip a longe line on him," said Madison. "But you're in charge. I'm here for backup only."

She helped Paley mount and spent a few moments correcting her posture. "Sit tall. Tight stomach. A little more curve in your lower back.

Heels down. Super." Madison patted Paley's knee. "How do you feel?"

"Afraid to move?" Paley offered.

Madison chuckled. "You're funny."

"I'm serious."

"Keep that shape in your body but relax into it a little," Madison said, flipping her ponytail over one shoulder and moving away from Prince and Paley. "You're going to get him moving with that same tongue click we've been using."

Paley couldn't believe how tall she was up on Prince's back. Everything looked different. The ranch spread out below her like a blanket of green. She could practically touch the clouds.

"Look where you want to go, squeeze with your legs, and click. If he still doesn't move, give him a nudge with your heels."

It felt right—so very right—with the sun shining and the creek singing next to them. Paley wanted to be part of it all. She shifted her weight forward, and Prince eased into a gentle, rolling walk. A surge of exhilaration swelled in Paley's chest.

Maybe Ma Etty was right.

Maybe Prince was the right horse after all.

CHAPTER THIRTEEN

Three days later, Madison decided they were ready to join the others.

"Prince will be more stubborn around the other horses," the trainer explained, "so you have to be more confident."

Paley's stomach clenched. "Can't we wait until tomorrow? I wanted to take Prince across the stream today."

"Sorry, sister," said Madison, shaking her head but looking sympathetic. "You can't hide out forever. Besides, Prince is ready for his debut at the ball."

Paley looked at her beautiful horse again. He wanted to strut his stuff. How could she deny him that? She took a deep breath, sat tall in the saddle, and directed Prince toward the big arena before she could change her mind.

It wasn't that she was scared exactly, but she didn't want anything to change with Prince. When they worked together down in the cottonwoods, they were connected. The golden thread shimmered between them, making everything sparkly and fresh. It was her own secret magic, and Paley was afraid to jinx it.

The arena was full of kids and horses and noise—snorts and whinnies, squeaking leather, and above it all, the burble of voices. Prince's fluid stride changed, becoming more staccato. His ears flicked this way and that, like he was paying attention to everything but her.

Leila was riding Cupcake around a row of orange cones. Her back was straight, and she hardly seemed to be holding onto the reins at all. Cupcake wove in and out with careful steps. When they got to the end of the course, Leila asked Cupcake to trot. When she saw Paley, a huge smile spread across her face, and she waved.

A warm rush filled Paley, and she sat tall without even thinking about it. She really did want to ride with her friend. Bryce was up next, and when he rode past her, Prince gave a sudden, nervous step to one side, and Paley slipped on the slick saddle.

Maybe her horse was remembering the *squish-crunch* of the slap. Maybe *he* was afraid.

And her job as the rider was to make him feel safe. Prince might be huge and powerful and beautiful, but he needed her to be brave. *Confidence. Conviction. Courage.* That's what Fletch had said. Paley had to ride with the confidence of a warrior. She had to be Prince's queen.

Paley tightened her stomach muscles until she felt compact and sturdy on Prince's back. She ran her palms down his neck, trying to tell him with her body that she would never ever let anyone hurt him.

When Madison asked her to take a circuit around the arena, Prince moved into stride easily, and Paley let herself move along with him, matching the rhythmic rock of his gait. It was marvelous. On Prince's back, even walking felt like winning. She circled the arena, always looking the direction she wanted him to go, until she asked him to halt by Leila.

"I'm so glad you're here," said Leila. "Do you want to try the cones?" Paley nodded. "Remember to anticipate the turns," her friend said, "and then use the rein and your leg to direct him."

Paley traced the course in her mind until she felt sure that she knew what to do, then she gave Prince one more pat and asked him to walk.

In and out. In and out. Paley and Prince wove through the cones. One cone and then another. Paley focused harder than she ever had on plotting their trajectory through the course. When she reached the end and pulled Prince to a stop, she was thrilled and exhausted all at once. She let her breath out in a huff and leaned down to stroke Prince's powerful neck.

"Wow!" said Leila. "You're a natural. It takes some people forever to learn to ride like that."

Paley's cheeks practically hurt from grinning. "It's all Prince. He's amazing."

Leila put her hands on her hips and pursed her lips. "I know about horses, Paley Dixon, and no horse moves like that all on his own. You guys are a great team."

Prince shook his mane like he knew she was complimenting him, and both girls laughed.

"Let's do it again," suggested Paley, nodding for Leila and Cupcake to lead the way.

The third time through, they figured out how to do the course in formation. Both girls started at the same end of the line of cones. Leila and Cupcake went to the right. Paley and Prince went to the left. Every time their paths crossed, they high-fived.

\\\

As they rode toward the barn at the end of the lesson, Paley felt hot and sweaty and exhilarated. Leila talked a mile a minute about the plans she had for their next riding session. Paley half-listened as she used an old towel to dry off Prince's back, damp where the saddle had rested. She sprayed his mane with detangler and combed it until it shone.

"I'll meet you inside for lunch," said Leila, putting Cupcake in her stall.

"Burrito bar?" Paley asked.

"I think so."

Paley ran her hand along Prince's flank as she moved toward his tail. "I'll be in soon," she said, working on a snarl. Prince stood calmly as she worked. By the time she was done, both of them were blissed out. As long as she and Prince stuck together, they could do anything.

Bryce came in with the big red gelding that was even taller than Prince. He put the horse in the cross-ties without a word. Mechanically, he unsaddled the horse and gave him a cursory brushing. Paley watched him out of the corner of her eye. She'd noticed that ever since he'd hit Prince, either Fletch or Madison stuck close to Bryce. Paley was surprised to see him come in alone.

It made her nervous.

Paley was done grooming Prince, and the only thing Bryce had left to do was take care of his horse's hooves. Ma Etty was a stickler for foot care. Paley watched as he stood next to his horse, staring at the metal hoof pick in his hand. He shifted his weight back and forth.

Paley could feel his hesitation the same way she could feel when Prince was agitated. Not that she blamed him. It was scary to have a big old horse looming over you. Paley kept working on Prince's tail, even though there wasn't a single tangle left.

Bryce fiddled with the hoof pick until finally, he bent down, wrapped his fingers around the horse's ankle, and tugged. Nothing. He tried again. Still no response from the horse, who placidly swished his tail back and forth. The movement matched the back and forth swing of Bryce's head as he looked to see if anyone was watching.

Paley ducked her head to hide her face. There

was a glint in Bryce's eyes that made her stomach clench. His horse must have sensed something too, because he pulled back against the cross-ties.

Prince was ready to be turned out in the pasture. It would be so easy to lead him out of there, away from trouble. Paley itched to get out of the barn and away from Bryce, but then she thought about when he had hit Prince. No horse deserved that. She had to step in. Maybe Bryce wasn't planning anything bad, but maybe he was.

Prince blew on her cheek.

"I know. I know," she whispered. "I've got to stand up." She shook out her braid and took a deep breath. "Hey, Bryce," she said, walking over to where he stood, fist clenched around the pick. "Leila showed me this great trick for doing their hooves. It's way easier. You want me to show you?"

He squinted at her. Paley tried to look both helpful and nonchalant at the same time. Bryce frowned like he was figuring her angle, but he matched the nonchalance they were both faking. "You want to do it for me? Sure. Why not?"

She forced a smile and took the pick from his hand. Paley took a moment to say hello to the big red horse and show him the pick. When she moved into position, Paley started humming the opening music for *Dragonfyre*. It always made her feel brave.

"If you do this," she said, running her hand firmly from the horse's flank down the length of his leg, "he'll feel more comfortable." In just a few minutes, she had all four hooves cleaned and handed back the pick.

Bryce grunted something that Paley figured was supposed to be *thanks* and took the pick.

When she left the barn, her heart was still beating fast. She hadn't faced any goblin hordes or fought a fire snake, but she felt victorious just the same. She gave Prince a kiss on the nose before she turned him out into the pasture. After he had sauntered away, she raised her face to the sun and thought that Ma Etty was absolutely right.

Horses do make everything better.

CHAPTER FOURTEEN

A week later, Ma Etty woke everyone early by putting a tray of hot cinnamon rolls, bacon, and a thermos of cocoa in the bunkhouse.

"This is going to be the best day ever," said Paley, through a mouthful of icing.

"No kidding," said Madison, rubbing the sleep out of her eyes and cramming a slice of bacon in her mouth. "I love trail rides."

"And cinnamon rolls!"

Sundee pulled the blankets over her head. "It's too early," she moaned.

Madison uncovered her. "Come on, sleepyhead. Rise and shine before I eat all the cinnamon rolls."

The whole crew had been talking about the

ride for days. They were heading to a small lake nestled on the other side of Fool's Butte. Riding and swimming! It sounded like a perfect day to Paley. She finished getting dressed and went to sit on the front porch of the bunkhouse with her cocoa and three slices of bacon. In the east, the sky looked like orange sherbet. To the west, it was a deep, sleepy blue dotted with stars.

"That's some sky," said Leila, zipping up her jacket and sitting down.

"I never saw anything like this in LA."

"Did you meet any movie stars?"

Paley crunched on her last piece of bacon. "No. It's not really like that where I grew up."

They could hear voices and an occasional thud from inside the boys' bunkhouse.

"Hey, Madison," Leila called inside, "can we go tack up?"

Their trainer poked her head out the door. "Sure thing, girls. I'll catch up with you." As the door closed, they could hear her trying again to rouse Sundee. "Come on! If you don't get moving, you'll have to stay and muck stalls."

"Think she'll make it?" asked Leila, as the two girls headed for the barn.

"Yeah," said Paley. "She might like to sleep, but she doesn't like mucking stalls."

Dumpling and Hot Tamale—the real early birds—led the rest of the flock out of the chicken coop. Cameron was the only one in the barn. His brown and white pinto mare stood placidly munching grain while he brushed her. He started talking as soon as he saw them.

"Did you know that Paul's dogs know ten different whistled commands?"

"Really?" Paley asked, opening Prince's stall.

"Yeah. Isn't that cool?" When Cameron wasn't riding or weeding or playing chess with Mr. Bridle, he shadowed Paul, asking a thousand questions about ranching.

Prince nickered his *good morning* to Paley as she measured out his grain and gave him a little alfalfa. She stroked his neck and leaned into his flank. "Good morning, Your Majesty."

Before long, the rest of the crew joined them. Even Ma Etty and Mr. Bridle were going on this expedition. Everyone got a set of saddlebags to add to their horse's tack, and Ma Etty passed out lunch bags and water bottles. "Sunscreen?" she asked, checking in with each kid. "Towel? Swimsuit?"

Paley stowed her gear in Prince's saddlebags and tucked a few extra horse treats into her pocket. Today was wide open with possibilities.

\\

They followed Bridlemile Road deep into the heart of the ranch. When it veered off toward the west, Mr. Bridle led the way along a smaller path that led to the butte. After a few hours, they were on public lands, and the trail widened, making it possible for them to ride two by two.

The Bridles rode together at the front. Fletch brought up the rear. Paley nudged Prince into a trot until she was even with Madison and Snow White. "How much farther?"

The trainer pointed ahead to where there was a break in the ridgeline. "The lake is right through there. You're going to love it. I wish it didn't take so long to get out here. I would swim in the lake every day if I could."

Bryce had caught up with them. He and Madison fell into conversation about open water swimming versus pool swimming, and Paley zoned out, letting Prince slow his pace and grab a few mouthfuls of grass. Here the landscape was more wild. There was a spicy, fruity smell that she couldn't identify. A flash of movement in the aspens on one side of the trail caught her eye, and Paley turned in time to see a doe and her fawn leap away.

Nothing could be farther from LA—or farther from the Misery Marshes, for that matter. Paley found herself thinking less and less often about the Blue Elf or about the dragon's egg. Sure, she still wanted to fly, but there was time for that—plenty of time. Her days with Prince were numbered.

"I'm ready for that swim," said Leila, urging Cupcake forward. "It's getting really hot."

Paley grinned at her. "Me, too!"

"Should we ask Ma Etty if we can trot?"

Paley nodded. That was a great idea! They'd been working on trotting in the arena for the last week. Prince loved it. The faster, the better!

When they topped the next rise, Paley could see a sloping meadow stretched out between them and the shore of a glittering, turquoise lake. Ma Etty nudged her horse into a trot and the rest of them followed. The world around Paley turned into a blur of color, and laughter bubbled out of her. High on Prince's back, she felt like she could conquer the world.

When they reached the water, Ma Etty asked them to let the horses drink. Paley soaked in the sparkling day with Bryce on one side of her and Leila on the other. As everyone caught their breath, the quiet of the mountain lake was replaced by cheerful chatter. Paley wished the day could go on forever.

"Yay! Lunch!" said Leila, swinging down from Cupcake's back. "I'm starving."

The girls pulled their lunches out of their saddlebags. Ma Etty and Fletch spread out two picnic blankets. Leila, Paley, and Sundee sat on the red gingham one, and the boys joined them.

"What's this?" Mr. Bridle said, when he came over carrying his own sack lunch. "You young whippersnappers are taking my favorite blanket."

The kids exchanged nervous glances. Cameron started to get up, but Mr. Bridle chuckled and patted him on the shoulder. "Just kidding, young man. At ease. At ease." Mr. Bridle joined Ma Etty, Fletch, and Madison on the other picnic blanket. "I love these guys," he told Ma Etty. "They're good kids."

Lots of tiny wrinkles crinkled up around Ma Etty's eyes when she smiled at him. "The horses think so, too!"

"And we both know that horses are excellent

judges of character," Mr. Bridle replied.

Paley watched Prince nibble grass at the edge of the lake and felt that warm, connected feeling return. Mr. Magnificent sensed her watching and tipped his nose in the air. Who needed LA movie stars when you had a horse like Prince?

\\\

After lunch, the kids and Madison swam.

The first plunge into the cold mountain lake took Paley's breath away. She broke through the surface with her heart pounding in her chest and scrambled out onto a sun-warmed rock. Goosebumps rose on her arms and legs.

"What?" Bryce protested. "Giving up already?"

"It's cold!" Paley panted.

"You'll get used to it."

He and Madison took off in a swimming race across the lake, and Paley dove back in, splashing Sundee and Leila. She swam until her teeth started chattering and then dried off.

Ma Etty was reading. Mr. Bridle was snoring quietly, his cowboy hat tipped over his face. Paul and Cameron were working with the cattle dogs. The horses grazed together next to the glittering lake.

"It's like a travel brochure," Paley said to Leila, who sat next to her with her hair wrapped in a towel.

"I don't ever want to leave," Leila said, tipping her face toward the sun.

Paley's sparkle factor went down a few notches. "Ugh. Don't talk about that."

"You know," said Leila, propping herself up on her elbow and looking at Paley, "we can get together when we're back in Denver."

Paley grinned at her. "Seriously? That would be amazing!" She squeezed the excess water out of her braid. "But let's not talk about the end of summer. We've still got three and a half more weeks."

"Deal."

"Do you want to go exploring?" Paley asked, pulling a shirt over her swimsuit.

Sundee perked up. "I brought my geology stuff. There's a really interesting sedimentary formation over there." She pointed to the far side of the lake.

The eroded ridge of rock reminded Paley of a decaying layer cake, neither appetizing nor ripe for exploring, but she was in a good mood and the moldy cake was an excuse to walk around the lake in the sunshine. "Let's go."

"Did you reapply your sunscreen?" Ma Etty called as they got ready to go.

Leila waved a tube of SPF 30, and they took off, following a small game trail that meandered along the shoreline. Wildflowers bloomed on all sides. The day's soundtrack was all buzzy bees and the swish of grass and the voices of the others skittering over the water.

They left the trail and climbed uphill to the formation that Sundee wanted to investigate. The edge of it was slowly crumbling away. The base was littered with broken-off chunks of rock. Scree, Sundee called it. Paley's boots slipped and grated against the gravel as she climbed to the more stable top of the formation.

About the size of the horse arena, the rocky ledge stretched north away from the lake, ending in a steep cliff that overlooked the valley beyond. Here and there a few plants grew out of cracks in the rock, but mostly it was bare.

"Be careful of the edge," Sundee warned. "This sedimentary rock is not very stable. The lip could crumble."

"Okay, Mom," said Leila, wandering back into the meadow to make a daisy chain.

Sundee pulled out her rock hammer, broke off a chunk, and peered at it with the hand lens hanging around her neck on a cord. "Look at that grain size," she muttered and scribbled something in a notebook.

Paley stared off the edge of the cliff. Down below, cattle grazed near a patch of aspens. Two hawks soared back and forth in matched spirals. When they turned their backs to the sun, she could see how their golden-brown feathers gave way to a deep brick red.

Paley sat down on the rock and watched them, feeling the same calm that came over her when she and Prince were really in tune. It was like she was a part of everything. She'd fallen into the web of the place—wind on her face, sun on her back, horses at the ready. She ran her fingers over the surface of the rock, exploring all the little nooks and crannies. Absently, she hooked her fingers under a tiny ridge of rock and tugged. A slab about the size of a textbook gave way and came loose in her hands.

Paley turned the slab of rock over and over in her hands. It was a pale gray that reminded her of the pottery unit in her arts class back in LA. They'd started with hand-thrown platters and moved on to more complex, wheel-thrown projects. It had been satisfying to watch something take shape out of nothing. That was one of the things she liked about playing *Dragonfyre*, too. When you started the game, you had next to nothing—basic weapons, a leather vest, a tiny bag of gold coins. But if you kept playing, if you got good, you built an empire.

If only real life was so straightforward.

Paley hurled the slab of rock off the edge of the cliff and watched it whirligig through the air. When it smashed against the boulders below, it exploded in a whitish cloud of dust. Paley wedged her fingers under another lip of loose rock. It wiggled, but didn't come free. She squatted to get more leverage and pulled harder. A dinner-plate-sized piece cracked off. She hurled that one too, even farther than the last. As she watched it fall, the rumble of engine noise filtered up from below.

She'd know that Jeep anywhere.

When it pulled to a stop directly beneath her, Paley wasn't one bit surprised to see Thomas Goodstein get out and stare up at her. He didn't speak. Instead, he raised two fingers to his eyes then pointed them straight at her. His meaning was as clear as the mountain lake. *I'm watching you.* He and the other boys with him spread a map on the hood of the Jeep. After peering at it for a few minutes, they jumped back in the vehicle and roared off, leaving tire tracks crushed into the field of wildflowers.

Paley hefted the chunk of rock in her hands and threw it after the retreating vehicle. She missed by a mile. Stupid Thomas. Who did he think he was, giving her the stink-eye? She was still stewing when she noticed a dark bit of rock against the lighter stuff. Paley touched it and bent closer. At first the new rock had looked black, but now she could see that it was shot through with red and felt a little bumpy, like the skin of a mandarin orange.

Paley wedged her fingernails under the light rock and pulled up another chunk, revealing more of the dark rock. There was a lot of it buried under there. The shape of it made her curious. It wasn't jagged, but neither was it round like a river stone. The edge of it swooped like a frozen wave. It sent prickly feelings up and down her spine.

That meant something. But what?

Paley wanted to see more of it, but the covering layer of gray stone was no longer budging. "Hey, Sundee," she called, "come check this out."

As soon as Sundee saw what Paley was pointing to, she began to bounce up and down on the balls of her feet. "Is that a coal deposit? That could be valuable." She sprinted forward and knelt next to Paley.

"Ohmygosh, ohmygosh," she twittered, waving her hands wildly. Paley stared at her. Sundee looked like she was about to twitch out of her skin.

"Is everything okay?" Leila called from down below. She had a daisy chain looped around her head.

"You're not going to believe this!" Sundee squealed, waving for Leila to hurry up and join them.

"What is wrong with you?" asked Paley. "It's just a rock."

"Just a rock?!" Paley thought Sundee's eyes might pop right out of her head and roll off the cliff. "It's not just a rock!" she shrieked. "It's bone! It's bone!"

"You don't have to say everything twice," said Leila, plopping down beside Paley. "Get a grip. Besides, bone is white, not black."

"Not if it's a fossil! Give me some space. I've got to clear away more of this shale." Sundee waggled her hands at them until they backed up, and then went to work with the rock hammer she carried. Flake by flake she chipped at the gray rock, blowing on it. As Paley watched, the shape emerged from the rock. First a long, narrow piece. Then another chunk, at a sharp angle to the first—a triangular section that seemed slicker and shinier than the others.

Sundee chipped off more gray rock and used her handkerchief to clean off a layer of dust. When everything was clean, her shoulders began to tremble. "You guys—" she whispered. Paley leaned closer. What she saw made her tremble, too. Never in a million years would she have expected this.

Embedded in the rock was an enormous tooth.

CHAPTER FIFTEEN

The Bridles practically had to drag Sundee back to the ranch. She would have chipped away at the fossil all night, and the rest of the kids would have stayed with her happily. They had agreed it must be a dinosaur tooth, based on the size. Back at the ranch, Paley paced around the kitchen of the big house. "I can't believe it!"

Sundee was giddy. "I know! We could be famous!"

"This is the coolest thing that has ever happened to me," said Bryce. "I wonder if it's a T. rex."

"Or a velociraptor!" suggested Paley.

Sundee ran her fingers through her long, dark hair. "Ma Etty will probably let me do some online research. I want to see if there are any other known

137

deposits in the area. I wonder if they've been carbon dated." Paley loved it whenever Sundee dropped into full geology geek mode. She didn't understand half the things Sundee was talking about, but the intensity reminded her of being so absorbed in *Dragonfyre* that it became reality.

Leila and Ma Etty returned from using the phone in the back office.

"Did you get through?" asked Paley, and Leila gave her the thumbs-up.

Leila's dad worked at the natural history museum in Denver. He wasn't a scientist or anything, but he did fundraising for them and planned big fancy parties for rich people in tuxedos, so he knew a lot of the scientists. She was pretty sure he could get them in touch with the head paleontologist at the museum.

"So," Leila said, pouring herself a glass of lemonade and sitting down between Paley and Bryce. "My dad said that he would contact Dr. Moore. If it's as big as we say—which, duh, it is—then it is probably very important."

"Yay!" said Paley.

"But—" Ma Etty interrupted, "he also said that we shouldn't excavate it any further."

"Why?!" Paley protested.

Sundee waved her hands around even more wildly. "Of course. Of course. They have to see it *in situ*. The context is so important to the science. I should have thought of that. I can't believe I kept digging."

Leila made a grumpy face at her. "Stop freaking out."

"What's *in situ*?" Bryce asked.

Ma Etty looked amused by all their hubbub. "It means 'in its place.' Scientists can learn a lot about a fossil by studying the way the bones are configured and what kind of rock surrounds them. Leila's dad is going to call us back. The museum people may want to make a trip out here and check it out. Maybe even do a professional excavation."

"Maybe?" asked Paley. "What if they don't? Then do we dig it up ourselves?"

Ma Etty's lips pursed. "I'm afraid not. There are laws against that kind of thing."

The kitchen exploded in protests.

"But we found it!"

"We can't just leave it there!"

"It's ours!"

The older woman held up her hands. "Whoa, horsies. First things first. Let's find out if and when the paleontologist is coming out." The kids huffed into their lemonades. "I need all of you to help with dinner," Ma Etty continued. "Paley and Leila, can you set the table? Bryce, you're on salad duty. Sundee, potatoes need peeling. Cameron, can you go pick tomatoes?"

Grumbling, the kids went to work. Paley kept pausing, one hand on the forks in the utensil drawer, to daydream about the glimpse of skull. Not a dragon. Not a monster. Not a made-up creature. Long ago those sharp teeth had gnashed and clashed right here on Quartz Creek Ranch. Paley wanted to know everything about it. She wanted to turn back time and watch her dinosaur lumber through the thick vegetation of the Jurassic.

Leila nudged her. "Get moving, will ya?"

"Sorry." Paley followed Leila around the table, setting forks on napkins. "I just can't stop thinking about the dinosaur."

"Maybe Dr. Moore will bring out some of that imaging equipment," said Sundee. "You know, the kind that does underground radar detection."

Leila clinked her handful of silverware. "There might be more fossils."

"Oh, cool!" said Paley. "What if there is a whole herd of dinosaurs in the butte?"

Sundee looked up from her potatoes. "Predators come in packs, not herds."

Leila waggled her fingers in Sundee's direction. "A pack of dinosaurs? That doesn't sound right."

"It sounds wimpy," Bryce said as he tossed the salad. "It should be something scary."

Paley loved those crazy words for animal groups— a gaggle of geese, a murder of crows, and so on. "How about a devastation of dinosaurs?" she suggested.

"Or a destruction?" said Bryce.

"A dreadful!" offered Leila.

The back door banged open, and Cameron came in with a bowl of cherry tomatoes. "A dreadful what?"

"A dreadful of dinosaurs," Paley sang, pirouetting through the kitchen.

Cameron laughed out loud. "Don't they come in packs?"

Everyone tried to answer him at once. The kitchen bubbled over with excited conversation and the rich smell of Ma Etty's pot roast and garlic mashed potatoes. When Mr. Bridle came in, Paley danced over. "The museum people are coming to look at our dinosaur." The words died on her tongue. Lurking behind Mr. Bridle was Jim Goodstein, and he did not look happy. The lines around Mr. Bridle's eyes deepened. He gestured to Ma Etty. "We've got a bit of a situation here."

The kids fell silent.

Mr. Goodstein appraised Paley. She knew he'd heard her, but she didn't know what the look meant, only that it couldn't be good. She edged behind Mr. Bridle.

"Your kids have been causing trouble. Again," Mr. Goodstein announced. "Someone's been digging things up."

Ma Etty crinkled her brow. "I'm not sure I follow you."

"Holes!" he yelled, and Paley flinched. "There are holes on my property!"

"Let's talk on the porch, Jim," said Ma Etty, drying her hands on a dish towel.

He glowered at her. "Don't you try to shut me down, Henrietta. I know how you are about these children." He shook his hands toward the kids as if shooing them away.

Ma Etty let out an exasperated sigh. "Kids, you go ahead and serve up. Mr. Bridle and I will be a minute." She grasped Mr. Goodstein firmly on the elbow and turned him out of the kitchen.

He let himself be ushered out but craned his head around to offer a parting shot. "Stay off my land!"

Mr. Bridle pulled the door shut firmly behind them.

The kids shifted uneasily, listening to the rise and fall of voices on the porch.

"That jerk is as bad as his nasty old wife," said Bryce.

Leila went back to filling water glasses. "I don't know how the Bridles can stand having them for neighbors."

The other kids went back to their duties, still complaining about the Goodsteins, but Paley stood in the middle of the kitchen, unable to move. The Goodsteins thought she was a bad kid, and no amount of explaining would change their minds. It made Paley feel all shrunken up, like an apple left to rot.

CHAPTER SIXTEEN

The Fourth of July was Quartz Creek's biggest day of the year. People came from all over Colorado to watch the parade and go to the local rodeo. Paley was beyond excited.

The kids spent several days preparing for the festivities.

During morning riding lessons, Madison and Fletch had them practice riding in tight formation. Leila and Cameron were going to carry the Quartz Creek Ranch banner. Paley, Bryce, and Sundee would throw candy. They rode through the yard flinging cracked corn for the chickens so they could get a feel for it. On the day before the parade, Paul and Mr. Bridle drove ranch trucks beside and behind the kids so they could assess how the horses would react to blaring horns, exhaust fumes, and engine noise.

When the holiday finally arrived, Paley pulled out her new Western shirt—lime green with white piping and the most beautiful pearl snaps up the front—and her best jeans. She made sure her cowboy hat was dust-free.

"Do you want me to braid your hair?" she asked Leila, who had ditched her fancy English riding clothes for a Western getup as well. She'd even bought leather chaps with fringe all down the sides.

"Can I have a bunch of braids?"

"Sure, if you want to sit here all day," Paley said, laughing. "How about if I do two French braids instead?"

Leila settled down in the desk chair to get her hair done. "I wish my big brother could come to the parade."

"Why couldn't he?" Paley asked.

Leila sighed. "Mom signed him up for all these SAT study classes."

Paley thought about her own brother. The move had been a lot easier for him. Third grade was cake compared to sixth grade. Within a week, he seemed to have a million friends. Half the reason she buried herself in *Dragonfyre* was to escape the hordes of bratty boys that swarmed the house, shooting Nerf guns all over the place.

Madison came out of her room in a fringed Western shirt and jeans with sparkles down the legs. "Time to roll, cowgirls!" she trilled and shooed them all out of the bunkhouse.

They trailered the horses to the crowded staging grounds. Paley took in a whirlwind of color and noise. A vintage car club. A gaggle of old women dressed in purple. The high school ski team. A marching band. A bunch of preschoolers on tricycles. A flatbed truck entirely full of gymnasts in shiny red leotards. There was even a man riding a camel.

She went to work grooming Prince. "Looking good, Your Majesty," she said, and Prince huffed into her shoulder.

"Here's your parade saddle," said Ma Etty, hefting an amazing concoction of tooled black leather with small silver plates embedded all around the edges. "This belonged to Mr. Bridle's great-grandfather, the one who first homesteaded in Quartz Creek. It's a beauty, isn't it?"

Paley thought her heart might burst. It was a saddle fit for royalty. "It's incredible."

Ma Etty helped her tack up Prince and filled the saddlebags with hard candies. "Mount up so I can adjust the stirrups for you."

On Prince's back, the view was even better. Behind them the town fire trucks had joined the queue. Up in front came the Quartz Creek Cattle Queen and her court of Cattle Princesses. People lined the main street of town. Kids bounced around like popcorn popping. The sun was high, and it was a glorious day for a parade.

Leila and Cameron rode into position. Paley and Sundee flanked Bryce. Fletch and Madison rode behind them, and the Bridles brought up the rear in an antique, horse-drawn buggy.

Five minutes until start time!

People kept coming up to the Bridles, hugging them and complimenting Paley and the others. These were good people—horse people like the Bridles—who took care of their animals and worked the land. Paley couldn't have felt farther from LA, but she realized she liked it. No wonder Fletch had left New York City to stay here for good. This was amazing.

Even the Blue Elf would agree.

The Master of Ceremonies rang a giant-sized cowbell, and slowly the parade began to move forward. Prince tossed his mane and high-stepped in royal style. Paley threw candy and waved until her arms were exhausted.

A few blocks from the end of the parade route, she was hot, sweaty, and nearly out of candy. Her cheeks hurt from grinning at all the little kid faces shining up at her, but she would have done it all over again in a heartbeat. As she threw her last handful of candy, Paley caught sight of Thomas Goodstein and his gang, lounging on a bench in front of the rock and mineral shop.

A sneer twitched on the edge of his thin lips when he saw Leila and Cameron carrying the ranch banner. He pushed off the bench and shoved his way through the little kids on the sidewalk. When he caught Paley watching, Thomas pushed his Indiana Jones hat back on his head and winked. Not in a nice way. He cupped his hands around his mouth and yelled, "Hey, everyone! Public service announcement. Delinquents ahead. Watch for poisoned candy. Protect your kids!"

His words cut through the joyous commotion of the parade like a sword to the heart. Paley turned to concrete on Prince's gorgeous parade saddle. She wasn't even sure her heart was still beating.

She couldn't ride past Thomas Goodstein. She just couldn't! Immediately, Prince balked and sidestepped. Sweat trickled down the side of Paley's neck.

"Come on," Bryce said through clenched teeth. "Let's get this parade over with so I can beat his stupid face in." But when Paley tried to urge Prince on, he refused to move. Bryce was beet-red and halfway out of his saddle. Behind them the whole parade was grinding to a stop. The Quartz Creek Cattle Queen and her court kept moving. So did Leila and Cameron with the banner. The gap between them and Paley grew every second.

Bryce and Sundee hesitated, unsure if they should stay with Paley or keep going.

"Get moving!" snapped Sundee. "You're not doing it right."

"Look the way you want to go," said Bryce.

Paley had the reins too tight and nudged Prince with the wrong leg. Her body was rigid and unbalanced. Prince twitched beneath her. The fire trucks behind them were honking. The parade-watchers on either side of the road had started to notice the problem. Paley was a rock in a stream, holding back the flow. She was sure that any second now Prince would run pell-mell into the crowd.

Thomas and his friends fell over one another laughing and pointing.

"Stay in formation," Madison called. "Let's go."

Bryce urged the big red horse forward. He and Sundee were leaving Paley behind. "Come on," he called, twisting around in the saddle to look at her.

Panic rose in Paley. "I can't get him to go!"

"He won't go? Or *you* won't go?" Bryce challenged. "Let's show those Rock Hounds what's what. You found a freaking dinosaur. They can suck on that."

The dinosaur. That's right!

She had found a dinosaur. Those jerks could drive around looking for their stupid rocks, but she was the one who had found a dinosaur. Remembering the way the tooth curved to a deadly point sent a thrill racing through Paley.

"Be in charge!" Bryce said.

Paley fixed her eyes straight ahead, found her seat, and squeezed with her legs. Immediately Prince began to trot. She caught up with Bryce and Sundee. Bryce grinned at her and raised a fist in the direction of the Rock Hounds. Paley raised a fist with him.

She was not going to let Thomas and his stupid rock club ruin the Fourth of July!

CHAPTER SEVENTEEN

"**D**id you have fun?" Ma Etty asked them when the parade was over and they reconvened at the horse trailers.

Paley gave her the thumbs-up, even though she was still a little shaky from her run-in with Thomas Goodstein. Ma Etty held Prince's bridle while Paley dismounted. "Glad you liked it. The Fourth of July is my favorite holiday. I love the parade, and I love seeing old Mr. Crockett with that goofy camel of his." Several parking spaces over, the camel was chewing hay while its owner removed the animal's weirdly padded saddle and blanket covered with tassels.

After the horses had been untacked and brushed

down, Ma Etty gave the kids permission to wander through the parade grounds. "It will take us a while to load the horses," she said. "Be back here in forty-five minutes, okay?"

Sundee and Cameron went to check out the rock and mineral shop. Bryce decided to stay and help with the horses. Paley and Leila beelined for Mr. Crockett.

"Do you think it will spit on us?" Leila said as they trotted over to the camel.

Paley made a face. "Do they really do that?"

"They do," said the old man, greeting them with a wide grin that turned his face into an entire landscape of wrinkles. "And it does not smell very good. You must be Ma Etty's new batch of kids."

Paley squinted at him, but she could tell right away that, unlike the Goodsteins, he didn't think there was anything wrong with being Ma Etty's kids.

"Can we pet him?" she asked.

"It's a her. And yes."

Paley patted the animal's thick, wooly coat. Leila stroked its nose. The camel blinked its long eyelashes at them and wiggled its flubbery lips.

"Um . . . Mr. Crockett?" Leila asked. "Why do you have a camel in Colorado?"

"Why not?" he chortled. "Everyone else has got horses, and jackalopes are too small to ride."

The girls laughed. Quartz Creek was definitely wacky, but in a good way.

After they said good-bye to Mr. Crockett, Paley and Leila went to buy elephant ears. Once they each had a piping hot, cinnamon-and-sugar covered pastry, they wandered through the staging ground to watch the rest of the parade marchers packing up.

The gymnasts were doing handstands on the back of their flatbed truck. Beyond them, Paley caught a glimpse of the Rock Hounds. The boys huddled together in front of the Jeep, listening hard to Thomas. He was leaning in and talking too low for Paley to hear anything. Every few words, he glanced around as if checking for listening ears.

Paley held one finger to her lips and gestured for Leila to follow. Together, they sidled closer, edging behind one of the classic cars from the parade.

"I still can't hear anything," said Leila, frowning. The packing-up noises of the marching band and the stomping, snorting horses that were tied to nearby trailers made eavesdropping impossible.

"We've got to get closer." Paley pointed to a

long pink Cadillac parked close to where the boys were talking.

They took cover behind the tuba players lugging their huge instrument cases and snuck over to the car.

"It's risky," one of the boys said. "Is he paying enough to make it worth our while?"

"Is it enough?" Thomas looked incensed. "Did you not hear what I said, idiot? The collector will pay at least five grand. More if it's complete."

Paley and Leila exchanged a look.

"So you really think she found what she said she found?" asked another boy.

"I know she did. I've been there."

The other boys looked dubious. "She took you?"

"Of course not," said Thomas, "but I always thought that the outcrop by the lake looked promising. I saw all them ranch kids over there, and Gramps told me what he'd overheard at the Bridles'. I put two and two together. Sure enough, when I drove out there, I found it."

Leila squeezed Paley's arm. Paley felt like she might puke.

"All we have to do is dig the thing up," Thomas continued.

"How long do we have?"

"A couple of weeks until the collector gets here."

The first boy shook his head, looking worried. "I don't know. Isn't it on public land? That's a whole different game than digging on your grandparents' property."

"Hardly anyone ever goes up there," said Thomas, drumming his fingers against his leg. "All we need is a good excuse."

Another boy grinned and rubbed his hands together. "No reason we can't be doing a little bird-watching on public lands, now, is there? I've always wanted to see a green-footed poppycock." He held up his hand, and Thomas Goodstein smacked it with his own, grinning. "Come on," said Thomas. "Let's head back to my grandparents' house. They're roasting a whole pig tonight."

The Rock Hounds pounded one another on the back and roared out of the fairgrounds. Paley slumped to the ground behind the Cadillac.

Dumb, stupid boys.

Leila squatted beside her, patting Paley's shoulder and chewing on her fingernail. Paley wanted to scream. If she were like Bryce, she could have plowed Thomas's stupid face into the ground. But she wasn't like Bryce.

"It's mine," Paley said, hitting her fist on the hard, dry ground. "Mine!"

"I know!" said Leila.

Paley threw her hands in the air. "What are we going to do?"

\\\\\\\\\\\\\\\\\\\\\\\\\\\\\\\\\\\\\\\

The girls raced back to the trailers and arrived hot and sweaty.

"Mr. Bridle! Ma Etty!" Paley panted, pulling on their arms. "It's a disaster!"

"You've got to do something," Leila said.

The other kids crowded around them, clamoring to know what Paley was so upset about. Ma Etty shushed them. "Now, Paley," she said, furrowing her brow. "What's wrong, honey?"

"I . . . we . . . I mean . . . Leila and I heard that Goodstein boy talking to his mean friends."

Bryce leaned closer. "What did he say this time?"

"They found out about the dinosaur, and they want to steal it."

The kids erupted in protests, and people nearby turned to look at them. Paley covered her mouth. The last thing they needed was for more people to know what they'd found. Ma Etty's concern had morphed into a frown. Mr. Bridle didn't look too pleased either.

"Were you spying on them?" he asked.

"No!" said Leila.

Paley dropped her hand from her mouth. "Kinda. They looked like trouble. So we listened in." Ma Etty shook her head. Paley's spluttered protest stalled out at a stern look from Mr. Bridle, but Leila jumped into the fray.

"You weren't there! You didn't hear them. We did. That awful Mr. Goodstein heard Paley talking about the fossil. Remember?" The circle of kids clustered around them nodded.

"And Thomas saw us at the lake," Paley added.

"He's no dummy," said Leila.

"I don't know about that," Bryce muttered.

"Calm down," said Ma Etty. "Even if Thomas knows about the fossil, what makes you think he plans to steal it?"

"He said a collector offered him $5,000 for it!"

Bryce let out a low whistle. The Bridles exchanged a look.

"Do you think—?" Ma Etty began.

Mr. Bridle pushed his cowboy hat back on his

head. "Unlikely. I don't see as how a couple of boys could make off with a fossil of that size. I'm pretty sure excavations like this take a long time."

"They could be fast if they ignore the site integrity!" Sundee said.

Her earnestness made Mr. Bridle smile. "My guess is that Thomas and his friends are full of big talk and not much action."

"The fossil is on public lands," Ma Etty added. "There are very strict laws about that. As persnickety as the Goodsteins are about property lines, I don't think they would condone any violations."

"But—" Paley protested.

Ma Etty patted her on the shoulder. "Right now we need to get these horses back to the ranch. We can talk more once we're home." She gave Paley one more squeeze and then shooed everyone into the van. "Come on, crew. Let's roll out of here."

That was that. Conversation ended. Case closed. Paley climbed into the van, deflated.

"I'll call my dad again as soon as we get back," said Leila, turning around and leaning over her seat to talk to Paley in the back. "Maybe he's heard from Dr. Moore. Maybe she's coming soon."

"Maybe," said Paley. But probably not.

Sundee frowned at her. "You sound like you've already given up."

Paley shrugged and moved into the backseat of the van as far away from the rest of them as she could manage. She didn't want to give up on the fossil. Finding it was the first thing that had ever happened to her in real life that was more exciting than her adventures in *Dragonfyre*. She wanted, more than a dragon's egg even, to know what kind of fossil it was and how much of the skeleton was there and whether it was something new to science.

But in real life, she was only a kid without any of the skills or magic of *Dragonfyre*. All a kid could do was wait around for adults to do stuff, and they hardly ever did the stuff they promised anyway. Paley couldn't save her fossil any more than she had been able to make the boys in the gamer club accept her. It was going to slip through her fingers like her life in LA and everything else that had mattered.

CHAPTER EIGHTEEN

To make everything worse, when they got back to the ranch, Prince refused to listen to anything Paley said. Fletch and Madison had to get him out of the trailer and into his stall. He balked when Paley tried to groom him, and finally she gave up. After she'd filled his grain bucket and refreshed his water, Paley sat in the barn on a mounting block with her chin in her hands, moping.

"There you are," said Leila, pushing open the barn door. "I've been looking for you." Paley gave her a halfhearted wave. "I talked to my dad again," Leila continued. "He said that Dr. Moore is on a dig in Mongolia or something and won't be back for a week."

"Great," said Paley, sounding anything but great.

"But—" Leila went on, trying to nudge Paley out of her gloom, "he e-mailed her and she replied. They will both drive down when she gets back and check it out. Two weeks, tops."

Paley picked at a piece of hay until it disintegrated in her hands. "Two weeks? That's when Thomas said the collector was coming."

"I told him that, too. My dad said not to worry because excavating a fossil takes way more time than that. Months, sometimes!"

"Then why did Thomas seem so sure that he could have it ready for the collector?"

Leila threw up her hands and paced around the barn. "He's bragging like a dumb-head."

Paley made a face at her. "Dumb-head? What kind of an insult is that?"

"I don't know!" said Leila, letting out an exasperated breath. "A dumb-head one. Now, come on." She tugged on Paley's arm. "We're supposed to help make dinner."

At the big house, Cameron and Mr. Bridle were finishing a game of chess, and Sundee was making plans with Madison to tie-dye shirts the next day. When dinner was ready and everyone had taken their place at the table, Ma Etty made them hold hands. Bryce protested, but eventually he took Paley's hand, and Ma Etty began, "Today at the parade, you all made me and Mr. Bridle very proud. We love the way you have come together as a team, as friends, as good people. Thank you."

Madison gave a little cheer. On Paley's other side, Paul squeezed her hand.

"Take a moment," Ma Etty continued, "to give yourself a little pat on the back for a job well done."

Bryce dropped Paley's hand like it was on fire and made a show of smacking his own shoulder. Everybody else laughed, but Paley stared at her plate. A job well done? Nothing would be *well done* about this summer if she let Thomas get to the dinosaur. She had to do something.

But what?

Even now, he might be up at the lake, hammering away at the rock that protected her fossil. Paley imagined the clink of metal against stone and the scrape of chisels inching her fossil out of the ground.

Every second, it was slipping through her fingers.

"What do you think, Paley?" Cameron nudged Paley out of her thoughts.

"Huh? What?"

"Leila was saying that she thought it would be

fun to ride a camel," Sundee repeated in her best know-it-all voice. "How about you?"

Paley grasped at the conversation around her. "Camels? I don't know. They're not really my thing."

"No camels in *Dragonfyre*?" Bryce muttered.

"No, there aren't!" she snapped. Her words came out more loudly than she meant them to, and all around the table, kids and adults fell silent.

Bryce rolled his eyes. "You don't need to get all touchy about a camel."

"I thought it might be fun to be up so high," said Leila, trying to smooth things over.

Paley slammed her fork on the table and shoved her chair back. "How can you all sit here and act normal when Thomas Goodstein is probably stealing the dinosaur right now?!"

Everyone stared at her.

Finally Mr. Bridle said, "Why don't you sit down, Paley? We're not done with dinner yet."

Paley's hands clenched into fists. "I'm not hungry, and you should be calling the sheriff instead of blabbing about some stupid, stupid camel."

Mr. Bridle raised one eyebrow and seemed about to say more, but Paley stomped toward the door and slammed it on the way out.

Ma Etty found her in the bunkhouse, flipping through the pages of her *Dragonfyre* book. Without a word, she set a big fat book on the table and sat down.

"What's that?" Paley asked.

Ma Etty pushed it toward her.

A glossy black skull with empty eye sockets and intimidating teeth stared at Paley from the cover of *Fossils of the Colorado Plateau.* "I thought you might find this interesting."

Paley set aside the *Dragonfyre* book and pulled the dinosaur one toward her. A painting at the very beginning depicted ancient Colorado as a giant swamp. Water stretched away into the distance. Strange plants held all manner of odd creatures. Paley flipped through to a map of current dig sites in the state, but there wasn't anything very close to the ranch.

"Thanks," she said, tracing the Colorado River across the map.

"I understand that you're concerned," said Ma Etty, "but maybe you don't need to fret so much. Your dinosaur has been in that cliff for millions of years. I don't think he is going to run away on you."

"I heard Thomas say he was going to steal it," said Paley, refusing to meet Ma Etty's eyes.

"I've known Thomas for his whole life. He is always putting on britches that won't stay on his behind."

Paley scowled. The last thing she wanted to think about was Thomas Goodstein's butt.

"Think about this logically," Ma Etty went on. "Why would an adult make a deal like that with a kid, especially if it's illegal?"

"I don't know, but we have to do something."

The older woman tucked a gray curl behind her ear. "What do you propose?"

"You should call the police."

Ma Etty patted her hand. "And tell them that one of my kids overheard another kid being a big shot?"

Paley bit her lip.

When Ma Etty put it that way, it even sounded dumb to Paley, but there had to be something they could do. In-game there was always a work-around. There was always another strategy.

"Let's call the news people," Paley suggested. "They'll probably want to do a big story. All the publicity will scare off the collector."

Ma Etty looked dubious, but she went along with

Paley. "All right. Why don't you write a press release tomorrow and send it to the local paper?"

"The paper isn't enough. We need TV. Reporters! Cameras!"

Ma Etty chuckled. "I guess you'd better make it a very compelling press release."

"Don't laugh," Paley muttered.

"Oh, honey," said Ma Etty, standing up, "I'm not laughing at you. I just think you might be making too big a deal of this." Long after Ma Etty was gone, Paley moped on her bunk, but eventually she pulled out a notepad and started to write.

CHAPTER NINETEEN

The next morning, Paley stood in the office as Ma Etty rummaged through the desk drawer for a stamp so she could put her press release in the mail. Every morning after that, Paley read the police blotter in the paper and checked the classified ads for suspicious "rock sales" and waited for reporters to call. They never did. Neither did Dr. Moore. Stupid Mongolia.

Paley sulked through her riding lessons, and the other kids, sensing her grouchy mood, gave her a wide berth. One afternoon as she walked to the end of Bridlemile Road to check the mail, Paley heard the rumble of an approaching vehicle and stepped off to the side to let it pass. The truck roared toward the Goodsteins' with what looked like construction equipment packed in the bed.

Moments later it was followed by Thomas in his jacked-up Jeep. He slowed and leaned out the open window. "Finally getting smart and running away, are you?"

Paley started walking.

He put the Jeep into reverse and backed up alongside her, matching her speed. "I get it. I really do. Old Man Bridle is no fun at all. No sirree."

"Leave me alone," said Paley, jamming her hands in her pockets.

"What?" Thomas said. "Just being neighborly. Wanna ride?"

His oily voice slithered over her, and Paley shuddered. "I'm fine," she said, even though her stomach churned. The thought of Thomas Goodstein getting a hold of the dinosaur made her sick.

"Suit yourself." He shrugged as if to imply that she was the rude one, and shifted the Jeep out of reverse.

As he engaged the clutch, Paley blurted, "I know what you're doing."

The Jeep stopped.

He stared at her for a long moment, a flicker of worry in his expression. "You do, huh?"

She jutted out her chin and stared back.

Thomas Goodstein regained his signature sneer and dismissed her with a wave of his hand. "I don't know what you're talking about. See you later, twerp," he said, roaring off in a cloud of dust.

When Paley had coughed the last of it out of her lungs, she sprinted back toward the ranch. The Bridles didn't think Thomas could steal an entire dinosaur, but Paley was pretty sure they were wrong.

She had to find a way to check on the fossil.

\\

The next day when Paley was cleaning Prince's tack after lessons, Fletch and Paul came in to fetch their horses.

"Where are you guys going?" she asked as they tacked up.

"We've got to move some cows," said Paul.

Paley put away the metal polish and had taken a few steps toward the door when the spark of an idea flickered. "Are you heading out toward the lake?" she asked, as casually as she could.

"Same direction," said Paul, "but not that far."

Paley shoved her hands in her pockets. "Need any help?"

Fletch watched her over Sawbones's back.

"Well, now," said Paul, tipping back his cowboy hat. "That's a nice offer, Paley, but we're going to be out for a while. You'll miss free time."

"Oh, I don't mind." Paley tried not to look at Fletch. "How about if I tack up Prince?"

"How about if you come clean?" said Fletch.

"What?" Paley asked, trying to sound as if she had no idea what he was talking about.

Fletch frowned at her. Paul scratched his ear, looking confused.

"There won't be time to check on the fossil," said Fletch. He might as well have stomped her into a pile of horse poop. Paley felt like she might explode from frustration. Fletch shrugged at her. "Paul and I have work to do. I'm not sure what you're planning, but I really can't risk you running off on me."

Paley spluttered out a stream of excuses and felt her face turn hot.

Fletch looked like he understood. "I know this is important to you, and I'm glad you're fighting for it." As Paul led the horses out of the barn and whistled for the dogs, Fletch turned back one more time.

"Try to be patient and wait for your paleontologist."

Paley slumped against a bale of hay. By the time Dr. Moore arrived, Paley was sure it would be too late.

\\

After they left, Paley wandered out to the arena, where Leila was playing soccer with Cupcake. Madison had given her a large exercise ball, the kind people use to do sit-ups on at the gym. It was hot pink and about three feet in diameter.

"You want it," Leila said to Cupcake, holding out the huge ball. "I know you do." The pony splayed her legs wide and put her head down, watching in rapt attention. When Leila booted the ball across the arena, it bounced wildly, sending up puffs of dirt, and Cupcake jumped into action. She raced across the arena, thrashing the dirt. Once she was close to the ball, she wheeled around and kicked out with her rear legs, sending the ball flying back toward Leila.

Perched on the top rail of the arena fence, Sundee laughed so hard she almost fell off. Paley climbed up next to her. Leila kicked the ball again. Cupcake flew after it, walloped it with one hoof, and turned to watch it career against the arena fence. When the ball finally rolled to a stop, Cupcake trotted up to it and nudged it gently with her nose.

Panting hard from chasing Cupcake, Leila jogged over to Paley. "Isn't she funny?" she asked, pointing to the pony.

"Yeah," said Paley in a downtrodden voice.

Leila wiped her face. "Man, you're grumpy."

Paley shrugged. "Have you heard from Dr. Moore?"

Her friend held up empty hands and said, "Mongolia," like that explained everything.

"This fossil is probably more important than whatever she is digging up right now," Paley protested. Leila nodded in agreement. "She's going to be too late!" Paley said, kicking the fence and nearly toppling Sundee.

"Watch it!" she snapped.

"Sorry," said Paley.

Sundee gave a tiny squeal, and Paley looked up to see Cameron and Bryce rounding the corner of the barn. Sundee waggled her fingers at Cameron, who immediately turned red. Bryce rolled his eyes. Paley gave them both a halfhearted wave.

"The fossil will be gone by the time I get back there."

Leila's forehead crinkled. "Do you really think so?"

"I don't know," Paley said. "Thomas seemed pretty confident."

Bryce leaned on the fence next to her. "He'd be an idiot to brag about all that money if he couldn't produce it."

Paley perked up. "So you agree with me?"

"It's one thing to brag about something no one can prove, but if he's promised the Rock Hounds all that cash . . ." Bryce held up his palms as if the situation was dead obvious.

"Maybe you could put signs all around the fossil," said Sundee.

Paley squinted at her. "What kind of signs?"

"Oh, you know," she said, smiling at Cameron. *"This site protected. Illegal to remove fossils from public land.* That sort of thing."

Bryce rolled his eyes. "We need a better plan than that. You might obey signs, but someone is stealing artifacts from public lands knowing full well it's illegal. Don't you remember that newspaper article Mr. Bridle read to us?"

"You're right!" said Cameron. "Someone had jackhammered a big panel of rock art."

Leila's eyebrows shot up. "And Mr. Goodstein said someone had been digging on his land!"

"Thomas is up to something," said Bryce. "No doubt about it."

Paley buried her face in her hands and groaned. "I've got to get out there."

"Go, then," said Bryce.

"How? I just asked Fletch and Paul to take me, and they said no."

"Hit 'em and take their horses." Everyone gaped at Bryce. "Just kidding," he said. "But seriously. You'd better figure something out."

"What about you? Don't you have any ideas, Mr. Big Shot?" Paley jumped down from the fence. This whole conversation was making her crazy. "Besides, I can't go out there alone."

"I'll go with you!" hollered Leila, as she tossed the ball for Cupcake again.

Cameron and Sundee agreed.

Bryce caught Paley's arm as she started to leave, and his earnest look surprised her even more than the contact. "We'll all go if you can figure out how to make it happen."

Make it happen.

Make it happen.

Bryce's words reverberated through her head for the rest of the evening.

After dinner and cleanup, Paley made her way to the barn with some extra carrots for Prince. She paused to say a quiet hello to Cupcake and the other horses. When she got to Prince, she held out a carrot, and he plucked it nimbly from her fingers with his flexible lips. She fed him another and opened the stall so she could go inside.

"Hello, Your Majesty."

He breathed on her cheek, enveloping her in the sweet smell of hay and carrots.

"I don't know what to do." Paley's voice cracked, and she pressed her forehead into Prince's neck. He nosed the pocket of her jeans looking for another carrot. Using the palm of her hand, she pushed his head away. "Watch it, Mister. You're supposed to ask nicely."

She froze in her tracks. Would that work? What if all she had to do was ask? Hope flooded her. It was worth a try. She kissed Prince on his big, soft nose and raced from the barn toward the big house.

Paley kicked her boots off on the back porch and made her way to the office, where Ma Etty was bent over the computer. "Still no news, honey," she said, when she saw Paley's expectant face. "You're just going to have to be patient."

Nervous energy jittered through Paley. She shifted back and forth, back and forth. *Confidence. Conviction. Courage.* That's what she had needed to work with Prince, and that's what she needed now. She took a deep breath. "Ma Etty, I really need to go check on the fossil."

Ma Etty started to respond, but before she could, Paley held up one hand. "Please hear me out." Ma Etty gave her one of those smiles teachers use when they are trying to be patient, and Paley kept talking all in a rush. "I know that you don't think Thomas can take the fossil, but what if he can? And what if we can stop it? The newspaper said stuff was getting stolen. Mr. Goodstein said there was digging on his property. What if Thomas is doing it? All you have to do is let me go to the lake. Everyone wants to go with me, and we can keep watch over the fossil until Dr. Moore comes and I know it's safe."

Paley clamped her lips shut, feeling her heart pound against her ribs. The noise of the computer fan seemed way too loud in the small office.

For a split second, Paley was halfway to the fossil. Prince was carrying her there at a gallop. In the next second, she knew exactly what Ma Etty was going to say, and it was like being thrown from his back.

"It's a half-day's ride to get to the lake. We have too much ranch business to take a full day off right now." Paley felt like the wind had been knocked out of her. "I promise that we'll go when Dr. Moore is here. For now, that will have to be enough." The old woman turned deliberately back to the keyboard.

The clicking of the keys filled the quiet house. Once Paley noticed the sound, it was all she heard. *Click, click, click.* Frustration roared through Paley. Why was it so hard to get people to understand her?

When her parents announced that they were moving, that was it. They didn't care about her opinion. She didn't get a vote. She got a big pile of boxes and was told to pack up her room. When she'd tried to join the gaming club, those boys hadn't even given her a chance to show her skills in *Dragonfyre*. She'd thought she was connecting with the people here, but even Ma Etty wouldn't take her seriously.

Click, click, click. The sound was all she could think about. The sound and what it meant to her. It was the sound of talons on castle walls and terrified livestock escaping. It was *Dragonfyre.*

Paley's fingers itched. If she could just get online for a little while, then it wouldn't matter that no one understood.

She could escape the waiting. She could escape Thomas Goodstein.

She could escape herself.

Click, click, click.

CHAPTER TWENTY

That night, Paley waited until the light streaming out from under Madison's bedroom door clicked off. She waited until Sundee was snoring like a little mouse. She waited until the world outside was still. A shiver raced through her as she slid out of bed. Part of the shiver was the cool boards against her bare feet. Part was the fear of being caught. Part was the anticipation of the journey.

Soon, very soon, the Blue Elf would be striding through the Misery Marshes, sword in hand, spell at the ready. There would be no Thomas, and even if he did show up, she could show him a thing or two. Pillar of Fire! Poison Miasma! There were so many options for revenge.

Paley eased the bunkhouse door open and slipped outside. The moon was past full and getting smaller every night, but it still illuminated the wide expanse between Paley and the ranch house. Night had transformed the familiar landmarks. The creek was liquid steel. The parking lot was a silver desert. The grassy pastures rolled like an ocean.

She'd forgotten shoes, and the gravel bit at the soles of her feet. Paley hop-stepped to the slick grass and made her way to the back door of the ranch house. She paused, one hand on the porch door, heart pounding.

Over the noise of the creek, insects hummed and chirped. An owl—at least she hoped it was an owl—called like some weird alien baby. A sleepy chicken gabbled some sleepy chicken dream from inside the coop.

And a door creaked open.

Paley froze, listening. The sound hadn't come from the house.

Feet crunched on gravel.

When the sound disappeared, Paley knew whoever it was had followed her across the lawn. The whispery swish of the grass came closer. Paley pressed her body against the side of the ranch house, wondering if her dark blue pajamas would camouflage her.

Nope. Leila rounded the corner and headed straight toward Paley. "What are you doing?" she hissed.

Paley exhaled. "Nothing."

Leila put her hands on her hips and tilted her head to one side. "Right. You're not doing anything in the middle of the night in your pajamas. Not one single thing."

"Be quiet. You'll wake the Bridles."

Leila's eyes sparkled, and she grabbed Paley's hand. "What's going on? Is it a heist? Are we taking down the Goodsteins? I'm ready!"

Paley's stomach flip-flopped. Leila seemed to really want to help, but she didn't realize it was too late for them to do anything. "Thomas Goodstein has already won," said Paley, wrenching her hand free.

Leila's face lost its sparkle. "I thought—"

"Just shut up, okay? You thought wrong." That came out louder than she meant it to. Her words hung in the air, ugly and irretrievable.

Leila's lip trembled. She clasped and unclasped her hands.

"Go back to bed," Paley said.

"Paley?" Leila pleaded, but when Paley refused to meet her eyes, she gave up and turned away.

Paley didn't bother to watch her go. There was no time to waste. She eased the back door open and crept down the dark hallway. The door to the office was ajar, and Paley slipped through, easing the door shut behind her.

She nudged the mouse, and the computer woke up. Ma Etty and Mr. Bridle were so trusting that they didn't even bother with user passwords on the desktop machine. Paley brought up a browser window and clicked through to the website for *Dragonfyre*. She'd have to download the program on the Bridles' crappy Internet connection before she could play. The status bar said it would take over an hour. The Bridles needed a serious speed upgrade.

Her knee bounced out a steady rhythm as she waited and waited and waited. After twenty minutes she heard a noise upstairs and held her breath, but before long everything was quiet again. She glared at the status bar, willing the download to go faster.

"Come on. Come on," she muttered at the screen. This was taking forever. And forever was long enough for her to start having second thoughts. *Maybe you shouldn't have yelled at Leila. Maybe you shouldn't break the Bridles' trust.* She crushed that internal voice. This was harmless, really. A little fun after the stress of the day. No harm done.

As the status bar approached 90%, her heart beat faster, abuzz with nervous energy. She pumped her fist at 100% and barely stifled a squeal when the program opened and prompted her for the login and password.

There was the Blue Elf, as tall and powerful as ever.

Her dark blue hair swooped as she turned and sprinted through the Misery Marshes. Her long legs sliced through the reeds as she headed for higher ground. The golden foxes lived in the Eivenwode. To retrieve the twelve hairs required to complete the task of the Elder Mage, the Blue Elf would have to find and kill one of the foxes. Paley couldn't take her hands off the mouse and keyboard long enough to cross her fingers, so she crossed her toes instead, and then crossed her legs for good measure.

The Blue Elf leaped to the top of a ridge for a better look at her path to the Eivenwode. It was night in-game, and the full moon gave her dark skin a silver sheen. It revealed her.

Arrows blasted past.

Paley winced. The Blue Elf crouched and, with a twist, flung herself behind a large boulder.

More arrows.

Paley's heart was racing now. The arrows were green-shafted and yellow-fletched. That could only mean one thing—goblins. The Blue Elf sprang into action. She had to run or she had to fight.

The Blue Elf always fought.

Paley's hands were sweating. Her attention was focused on the screen. The goblins crept along the rocks, mere smudges of gray in the moonlit night. She counted fifteen. The Blue Elf couldn't defeat them by sword alone. She prepared a Fire Spell.

Even as she watched the goblins move into fighting formation, Paley snuck a glance at the wall clock. It was after midnight. She couldn't believe how long she'd already been here and with so little progress.

At this rate she'd never make it to the Eivenwode.

The head of the last goblin rolled over the edge of the cliff, and the Blue Elf dropped her sword, depleted. Paley was panting and her hands hurt from playing for so long.

She rested her head on the desk.

Lack of sleep was catching up with Paley, and morning was getting closer every minute. She should go to bed, but this was her only chance to make progress toward the dragon's egg. Those stupid goblins had messed everything up. Now she would have to replenish the Blue Elf before she could go to the Eivenwode after the foxes. Paley pushed her exhaustion away and was about to get the Blue Elf moving again when the door behind her creaked open.

In the reflection on the computer screen, Paley could see Ma Etty in the doorway.

This was bad.

Paley considered bolting. But even if she could get past Ma Etty, where could she go? Instead, she spun slowly on the desk chair to face the old woman. They stared at each other for a long time.

Paley squirmed in place. Finally, she couldn't stand it any longer. "I'm sorry," she squeaked. "I couldn't help it."

Ma Etty shook her head a tiny bit and her normally laugh-happy eyes looked drowned. She might as well have stabbed Paley through the heart. Paley ducked her chin and waited for the yelling to begin. Still nothing from Ma Etty. Paley snuck a look and was surprised to see the old woman looking at the computer screen.

"Is that your character?" she asked, taking in the Blue Elf, who stood twitching in place without Paley to direct her. Her brilliant hair caught the moon. Goblin blood was smeared on her right bicep.

Paley nodded.

"She looks tough. I wouldn't mess with her." Ma Etty returned her attention to Paley. "Do you feel better now?"

That was the last question Paley expected, and she did not know how to answer. It had felt good. More than good. It had felt fantastic to play *Dragonfyre*, but now when the Misery Marshes were gone, replaced by the ranch office and the chirruping crickets outside, she wasn't so sure.

Nothing had changed. Thomas was still after the dinosaur, and no one seemed to really care. Correction. One thing had changed. She was in a heap of trouble. And Ma Etty still required an answer.

That whole *confidence, conviction, courage* business— it wasn't a one-time thing.

It was for always.

Paley stood up, stomach churning, and faced Ma Etty. "I don't feel better. Not at all." In fact, Paley thought she might puke on the office floor, a move which probably wouldn't help her out of this mess. "I'm really worried about the fossil, and I tried everything I could think of to get you to let me go out there."

Ma Etty's face softened. "And I still said no."

Paley chewed on her lower lip.

"That must have been very hard for you to hear," said the old woman.

Paley didn't say anything. Little by little, she was sinking into the floor, turning cave troll. Tomorrow she'd have to face Mr. Bridle. Everyone would know what she'd done. She didn't protest when Ma Etty took her by the arm and led her back to the bunkhouse. Paley climbed into bed and pulled the covers over her head.

She was never coming out again.

CHAPTER TWENTY-ONE

Birds started singing before the sun was even up. They were idiots. There was nothing to sing about. Paley's stomach hurt. Her eyes were red and scratchy. She'd hardly slept, and Mr. Bridle was waiting. She scrunched into the corner of the bunk and curled herself into a ball. Dumb birds.

Madison whirled through the bunkhouse flipping on lights, pulling off blankets, and talking about how they would be exploring knee guiding in the morning lesson. Leila made a point of not looking Paley's way, not even once, while she dressed. Even Sundee was up and dressed before Paley dragged herself out of bed.

During breakfast, Ma Etty talked to everyone but her. Mr. Bridle gave Paley a single eyebrow when he refilled his orange juice, and it was worse than a slap. As everyone was cleaning up, Ma Etty said, in a voice everyone could hear, "Paley, we need to see you in the office." The cheerful morning chatter vanished.

She and Mr. Bridle rose together and led the way toward *Internal Affairs*.

As Paley slumped after them, Leila met her gaze for the first time all morning. Her lip quirked up in a half-smile, a peace offering with sympathy on top. Paley's breath caught in her throat. Maybe there was still a chance to make things right. Then in another breath, Leila was gone.

Paley nibbled on a hangnail.

Ma Etty gestured for Paley to sit. "First, I want to say that I'm sorry for not listening to you, for not taking your concerns seriously enough. That was wrong of me."

Paley held onto the arms of the chair. "Really?"

"Really."

"But that doesn't mean that there aren't consequences," added Mr. Bridle.

Sounds from the arena filtered through the open office window. Panic spiked through Paley. What if her punishment was about Prince? What if she was going to lose him?

Mr. Bridle cleared his throat. "This ranch operates on trust. Ma Etty and I believed in you." Paley wished the floor would swallow her up.

"No riding," he said.

"Not forever," Ma Etty added, noticing the pained look on Paley's face. "Only for as long as it takes you to stack the load of firewood we're hauling in for the winter, and as soon as you're done, you can ride out to the fossil."

Paley leaped out of her seat. "For real? I can go?"

Ma Etty smiled.

Relief poured through Paley. She could stack wood. No problem. "I'll start right away!"

There was a loud rumbling on Bridlemile Road. Ma Etty headed for the door. "You're in luck," she said. "The firewood's here."

Paley flew to the back porch to get her boots.

"Lucky, lucky, lucky," she sang, as she raced around the house to join Ma Etty. She hadn't dared to hope that she would get off so easily. She could be at the fossil by midday.

Or not . . .

With a roar, the truck operator raised the rear compartment of the vehicle and dumped out the most enormous pile of wood. The heap was three times as big as the ranch van. It towered nearly as tall as the bunkhouse. There was enough wood to make a thousand campfires.

Paley's eyes swam with tears. "I can't do that! It would take me a year to move all that wood."

Ma Etty shrugged and said, "You'll have to figure something out."

\\\

By the time morning lessons were over, Paley had filled a five foot section of the woodshed. Her shoulders ached, her gloved hands burned, and she hadn't even made a dent in the pile.

"That's a ton of wood," said Leila, crossing from the barn to Paley's punishment zone.

Paley threw another piece in the wheelbarrow. "Maybe two tons."

"Bummer," said Leila. She seemed about to head into the bunkhouse when she turned around and faced Paley. "You know I didn't tell on you, right?"

Paley nodded and wiped the sweat from her face. "I know. I wrecked things all by myself. I'm good at that."

Leila shoved her hands in her pockets. "Well,

good luck," she said as she turned to go. Paley's heart ached. She had ruined a lot of things last night, but losing Leila's friendship was the worst.

She had to make things right.

"Leila," Paley called.

Her friend turned slowly. Paley's apology poured out. "I'm awful. I'm so sorry. I wish I could take everything back. I really want to stay friends."

Leila let out her breath and her face lit up. "I'm so glad. Me, too!"

"You forgive me?"

"It's not like I want to go on double dates with Cameron and Sundee."

Both girls laughed, and Paley got back to work with renewed energy.

"Do you really have to move all the wood?" Leila asked.

"If I want to be allowed to ride out and check the fossil, I do," said Paley, grasping the handles of the laden wheelbarrow and shoving it toward the wood-shed. By now the other kids had joined them. Bryce looked dubiously from the pile of wood to Paley's small stack in the woodshed.

"That's going to take forever," Sundee smirked. Cameron frowned at her and stepped away.

Paley finished stacking her load of wood and pushed the wheelbarrow back to the firewood mountain. She restrained herself from running Sundee over. Her back burned as she bent for another piece of wood. When she stood upright, Paley was stunned to see Bryce with a piece of firewood in each hand. *Bang!* Into the wheelbarrow went the first piece. *Bang!* In went the second.

She gaped at him.

"Don't get all lazy now!" he barked. "We'll never get done."

"We?"

He smiled at her.

"We!" said Leila, picking up a piece of wood. Cameron raced to the barn to find some more gloves, and even Sundee decided to help. By six o'clock, everyone was sunburned and aching, but the wood was stacked—enough for a thousand blizzards.

All through dinner, Paley jittered with the anticipation of tomorrow's trail ride, and she fell asleep to dreams of dinosaurs and flying horses.

CHAPTER TWENTY-TWO

Over breakfast the next morning, Mr. Bridle clinked his fork against his orange juice glass. When the hubbub around the table died down, he cleared his throat. "Ma Etty and I were pleased to see the way you worked together yesterday."

Bryce and Cameron raised their fingers in matching victory signs.

"Madison and Fletch report that you are all competent riders," Ma Etty added. "They need to help us with ranch duties today. But we've decided you can make the trail ride to the lake alone."

Cheers erupted from all sides of the table. Paley forgot all about her tight muscles and sore hands. They were going! They were really going!

Ma Etty handed them sack lunches. "You'll need to stick together."

"Horse safety comes first," added Mr. Bridle.

Cameron paused in front of him. "You mean horse safety comes before our safety?"

When the older man looked flummoxed, Cameron pointed fingers at him like six-shooters and said, "Checkmate, Mr. Bridle!"

Everyone laughed.

"Dinner will be at six. Get back by then," said Ma Etty, "and stay on our property until you get to the public lands. You know the fence line."

"Trust me," said Paley, clearing the table so they could get their show on the road. "The last thing I want is a run-in with the Goodsteins."

\\

Finally, they were off.

Paley nudged Prince into a trot, her body tuning in to the horse's rhythm. As she swayed in time with his steps, her muscles loosened up. It was a perfect summer day. Blue sky. Puffy clouds. A breeze rippled through Prince's mane.

And the dinosaur was waiting.

Paley itched to see it again, to run her fingers along the dark stone. "Let's run a little," she called to the other kids. Bryce let out a whoop and urged his horse into a canter. The five of them raced down the dirt road that ran along Quartz Creek. Everything was sun and sparkle and speed and horse. Paley had never felt so good in real life or in-game.

When they finally reined in and let the horses drink from the creek, Bryce had a huge grin on his face. "Man, I had no idea. No freaking idea."

"About what?"

"That this horse thing could be so amazing. I was so mad when my parents said I had to come here. I thought it would be like jail or that book where the kids have to dig pits all day long."

Paley stroked the side of Prince's neck. She loved him so much—his speed and his sass. Leaving him might break her heart. "We have to go home in a few weeks."

"That bites."

"Will you . . . I mean . . . do you think it will be different?" Paley asked, shading her eyes against the sun so she could watch his face.

"You mean, am I still going to beat kids up?"

She nodded.

He pulled a water bottle out of his saddlebag, drank, and handed it to Paley. "Here's the thing," he said. "Being like this, being friends, is better." Bryce spread his arms wide to take in Paley, the horses, the ranch, and the whole summer. "But sometimes there are people who deserve a good punch in the nose."

"Like Thomas Goodstein," said Paley.

"Especially him."

"But it's not nice to hit people."

Bryce snorted. "Are you going to work for Hallmark when you grow up?"

Paley rolled her eyes.

"I can't make any promises," said Bryce, "but I'm going to try to avoid firewood duty."

"That's a good motto," said Paley. "Let's make sure to tell that one to Ma Etty."

She and Bryce fist-bumped and then urged their horses onto the road with the others.

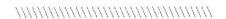

Even before Paley could see the lake, she knew something was wrong.

The sound of machinery thrummed through the

air. It made Prince uneasy, and Paley reined him in. The others gathered around her, straining to listen, trying to make sense of the sounds that came from just over the rise. A diesel engine spluttered and roared. The ear-piercing whine of a rock drill surged.

Her nightmare had come true. The fossil was being excavated.

The machine gave another roar, screeching as it bit into rock. Paley felt a stabbing sensation in her chest. They were going to take the dinosaur. She'd stacked all that firewood for nothing. They were too late.

The engine sounds cut off abruptly, and she heard rocks falling.

"Watch the end!" a man called. "Don't let that large section break off."

A younger-sounding voice responded. "Don't worry. We've got it."

Paley stared at her friends. "That's Thomas! I'm sure of it!"

They nodded, wide-eyed.

"I've uncovered another tooth," said a second boy. One of the Rock Hounds, no doubt. The kids could hear rocks being chipped away with some kind of metal hand tool.

"Could be an allosaur," said the man. "Not too shabby, especially because there's so much of it present."

"What now?" Leila hissed.

Sundee looked terrified. "We have to get out of here."

Bryce clenched and unclenched his fists, seething. Cameron fidgeted, twisting the reins of his horse back and forth in his hands.

Leila looked to Paley. "What do we do?" she whispered.

Panic filled Paley. She was supposed to do something, but what? The Blue Elf would . . . oh, who was she kidding? The Blue Elf wouldn't do anything to help because she wasn't even real. Paley was real, and she couldn't fight or cast spells. Nothing she tried to do came out right. They should turn the horses around and ride back to the ranch. They were too late.

The machine roared into action again.

"What's the plan?" Bryce asked.

Paley's grip tightened on the reins. She looked at her friends' tight, worried faces. They expected her to know what to do. They were counting on her. Going back was not an option. She had to come up with something, fast. Prince turned his head and snuffled against her leg.

His encouragement buoyed her up.

If they acted now, there still might be a chance of saving the fossil. It made her queasy to think about facing the Rock Hounds alone, but someone had to, and there was no Blue Elf. She would never forgive herself if she didn't try.

Paley pointed to her friends. "You guys have to ride back to the ranch and get the Bridles. We need their help."

Bryce's eyes narrowed. "What do you mean *you guys*?"

"You heard Mr. Bridle. Safety first."

He shook his head. "I'm not going anywhere."

"Me neither," said Leila, crossing her arms over her chest.

A surge of good feelings filled Paley. She'd never had friends like this before.

"We're staying," said Bryce.

"This is nuts!" Sundee squeaked. "You're going to get in huge trouble for this. And I'm not moving any more wood for you!"

Leila shot her a death glare. "Would you just shut up?"

Cameron nudged his horse next to Sundee's and leaned over until he could grab her hand. "Let it go," he said. "She's got to do this." To Paley, he said, "We'll go for help. Be careful, okay?"

Paley nodded, and they took off down the road. Part of her wanted to retreat to the ranch with Cameron and Sundee, but she was tired of backing down and giving up.

It was time to make a stand.

CHAPTER TWENTY-THREE

Paley got ready to lead Leila and Bryce into battle. "Are you ready?" she asked, choking back her own fear.

Grim-faced and determined, her friends nodded.

This wasn't going to be a Blue Elf–style blood-bath. It was a targeted strike.

"Okay," Paley said, keeping her voice steady, "we're going in at top speed. The goal is to shut down the machines. There's got to be power out there. We can try to pull the plug. But one way or another, we've got to get between the machines and the fossil."

"Got it!" said Leila.

Paley rolled her shoulders back and took a deep

breath. "Bryce and I will try to distract them. You sneak in on Cupcake. Let's go!" She tucked in and leaned over Prince's neck. Bryce did the same on his horse. Immediately, they shot forward, and the landscape was a blur on either side. Bryce angled to the right. Prince pounded to the top of the rise. When they crested it, Paley did not hesitate. She and Prince were a team, stronger together than either was alone.

They raced toward the Rock Hounds.

A man in a red T-shirt and protective goggles wielded some kind of a cross between a drill and a jackhammer. Nearly all of the fossil was uncovered. Long black bones shone in the sun, stark against the paler rock. The entire side of the skull was exposed, and several boys worked at it with picks and small chisels. Thomas sat on the hood of a truck with his thumbs hooked through his belt loops, looking like he'd just won the lottery.

When Paley and Bryce thundered into view, Thomas and the Rock Hounds jumped to their feet, and the man shut off the drill. Paley and Prince went full tilt until they were almost on top of the Rock Hounds. The boys backed up against the truck, mouths hanging open. Bryce rode around the far side of the excavation until the man with the drill was boxed in between the two horses.

The man swung the tool wildly from side to side. "Get away from me!" he cried.

Prince stamped and snorted.

"Get away from the fossil!" Paley said.

The man's eyes narrowed and he pointed the drill at them. "You kids are in the wrong place." There was no mistaking the threat in his voice.

Paley squared up her shoulders. "Excavating that fossil is illegal."

He snorted at her.

"This is public land," said Bryce, backing her up. "We'll tell the cops."

Thomas Goodstein had recovered from the shock of their arrival. "Nobody will believe them," he said, flashing an ingratiating smile at the collector. "They're delinquents."

Bryce stiffened.

A flash of movement caught Paley's attention. Leila had dismounted and was creeping behind the truck. Paley's heart thumped double-time. What if the Rock Hounds saw her? She had to hold their attention. "We've already told the museum in

Denver about the dinosaur," she said. "They're sending a paleontologist out."

The man's face turned a shade of purple.

"Impossible," sneered Thomas. "There are fossils all over these hills, and no one ever comes to check them out."

Leila was standing on tiptoes, reaching for the cord that connected the drill to the generator in the back of the truck.

"She's telling the truth," Bryce said.

The man pointed the spinning drill at Bryce and revved it up. The big red horse skittered and sidestepped. Even Prince was getting nervous. Leila had to shut that thing down!

The man turned on Thomas. "You told me this was your land."

"Close enough," said Thomas. A muscle in his cheek twitched.

The collector revved the drill in Thomas's direction. "You told me there was no way we'd get caught."

"Easy there," said Thomas, holding his hands out between them. "No one is getting caught. These kids can't do anything to us."

Paley's heart pounded against her ribs. Adrenaline

surged through her. She'd had it with people under-estimating her. She could ride Prince. She could join that gamer club. And she definitely could keep that awful man away from their dinosaur.

"Do it!" she yelled at Leila.

The plug popped free and the drill died.

"Get her!" yelled Thomas, spotting Leila.

Yells erupted on all sides. Bryce was half off his horse. The collector jabbed at the air with the long metal drill. The Rock Hounds scrambled after Leila.

"Leave my friend alone!" Paley shrieked. She shortened her reins and leaned into Prince. He stamped the ground and bellowed once, then the huge horse rose on his hind legs, pawing the air. When he crashed back down to earth, the force of his hooves made the ground shake.

Thomas turned white. The collector dropped the drill and ran for the truck. Bryce swung Leila up behind him on the saddle, out of reach of the Rock Hounds. Paley locked eyes with Thomas. "You're the one who has to go." Prince took a single step forward.

Thomas faltered. Fear flickered across his face. "Now," said Paley, pointing to the truck.

Thomas bolted, the Rock Hounds following reluctantly. The truck roared away.

Finally, Paley could breathe.

They had done it!

CHAPTER TWENTY-FOUR

Paley dismounted and leaned against Prince, feeling his strong, solid heat. She buried her face in his mane. There were no words for how much she loved this horse. He nickered and tried to nibble on her braid.

She laughed and held him tighter.

Leila and Bryce laughed too, relief flooding through them.

It was over.

"You were amazing!" Leila told Paley.

"It was all Prince."

Bryce ran his hand down Prince's flank. "But he did it for you."

Paley shrugged and grinned.

"What do we do now?" asked Leila.

"We wait for the Bridles," said Paley, starting to unsaddle Prince. The others followed her lead, and soon the horses were grazing on new grass next to the lake. After they ate their sack lunches, Bryce and Leila rolled up their pant legs and went wading. Paley lay back in the sun, watching a red-tailed hawk soar overhead.

Confidence. Conviction. Courage.

In-game or out of it, those were the things that mattered.

She tipped her cowboy hat over her face. The heat of the day enveloped her. Occasionally, a hint of breeze tickled her arms, but otherwise she was still, inside and out. Paley couldn't remember the last time she'd felt like this, cocooned by the knowledge that everything was right in the world.

"Paley—?"

She peeped out from under her hat.

Leila was staring down at her. "You were really brave."

Paley rolled up on one elbow. "I was, wasn't I?"

The Blue Elf couldn't have done better herself.

Paley's stomach was growling by the time they heard the noise of the ranch truck. She stood quietly with Leila and Bryce and waited for the Bridles.

"Do you think we're in trouble?" Leila asked.

Paley shrugged. "Probably."

Ma Etty jumped out of the truck and rushed forward to hug them. She put her hands on Paley's shoulders and turned her one way, then the other. "Are you okay?"

"Yes, ma'am. Prince wouldn't have let anything happen to me."

Mr. Bridle kept trying to look stern, but Paley could see a smile playing at the edges of his mouth. The last thing Paley wanted was to upset the Bridles, but she had to tell them what she intended to do next. Even if it made them mad.

"Mr. Bridle," she said, "I have to stay here. I hope you understand. Anyone could take the dinosaur now. It's not safe." Her throat felt tight with tears. Giving in, standing down, retreating to her cave— that had always been her approach when things got hard. It was so much easier that way. Standing up to the Bridles was much harder than facing the Rock Hounds. They'd been so kind to her. "You see," she stammered, "I promised myself that I would guard this fossil. I can't let anything happen to it. Not after what we've been through."

"That goes for all of us," said Bryce.

Leila stuck her chest out like she was ready for a fight. "We don't care if you call our parents or the sheriff or anything. We're not leaving until Dr. Moore comes and we know the dinosaur is safe."

Paley looked at her friends. Leila's skinny chicken arms were bent akimbo, and her hair had fallen out of her ponytail. Bryce had a big smudge of dirt on his forehead, and his face was flushed. Mr. Bridle cleared his throat. His eyes were glued to his boots. He shoved his hands into his jeans pockets. Probably he was getting ready to chew them out.

Paley braced for it.

But it was Ma Etty who spoke. "Cameron was pretty firm on that point too," she said. "That's why he and Fletch and the rest are coming with camping gear. If you feel this strongly about being out here, then we're going to be out here together. Now, who wants to get a campfire started so we can make dinner?"

\\

That night, they roasted corn and cooked hot dogs over a roaring campfire.

Everyone was there. Cameron and Sundee were sitting close together, holding hands. Paul played his banjo while Madison and Mr. Bridle sang. Fletch was teaching Bryce how to whittle, and Paley and Leila sat by the fire watching the flames flicker and the sparks dance in the night sky.

When the fire had burned down to glowing red embers, Mr. Bridle cut marshmallow sticks, and Ma Etty passed around graham crackers and chocolate. As Paley crouched by the fire, rotating her marshmallow over the coals until it was a perfectly puffed, golden-brown orb of goodness, she thought about how amazing it was to be here. Never in a million years would she have imagined such a night.

The dinosaur was safe.

The stars shone down.

She had friends at her side, and Prince was watching over them all.

CHAPTER TWENTY-FIVE

Paley adjusted the handkerchief over her mouth. The cattle-rustler look was supposed to protect her from rock dust. It also made her very, very hot and sweaty. It was almost three o'clock. Dr. Moore usually let them quit working mid-afternoon. On all sides of Paley, the other kids were showing signs of pooping out.

They'd been working on the excavation since nine o'clock, with only a short break for lunch. Tired as she was, Paley wasn't ready to stop. This was her last day—her very last day at Quartz Creek Ranch— and she still had so much to do. She bent over the foot she was uncovering and used a toothbrush to work around the smallest bones.

Ever since they had saved the dinosaur from the Rock Hounds, regular ranch activities had been superseded by work on the excavation. Dr. Moore said that this was the most complete allosaur ever found. Not just in Colorado. Anywhere! Sundee was beside herself with excitement.

All of them were.

Nothing like this had ever happened in Quartz Creek. They'd been in the paper twice and on the local news once. "Teens Find Terrifying Teeth," read one of the headlines. It was totally goofy and awesome. Leila worked next to her, and Bryce was on her other side. Paley wished she could stay here forever.

The Bridles and Dr. Moore rumbled across the scree in the Ranger and parked near the tent where the excavation team stored their equipment. They got out, carrying a cooler jug full of lemonade and a stack of cups.

"Break time," called Dr. Moore. She was a tall woman with aviator glasses and a long, dark ponytail. "Wow! You're making amazing progress." It was true. The kids, working closely with Dr. Moore's graduate students, had nearly finished the excavation. "I've got great news," Dr. Moore continued. "This baby is going to get the royal treatment at the museum. The installation will be right at the entrance, and we want all of you to be there for the big unveiling ceremony."

The kids cheered.

"Do I get to wear a tuxedo?" asked Cameron.

Dr. Moore grinned. "If you want."

Sundee made goo-goo eyes at him, and Leila and Paley fake-groaned.

"There's more news," said Ma Etty. "Turns out that there was an illegal fossil ring operating out of the rock and mineral shop in town."

Leila bounced with excitement. "Was there a sting? Did a SWAT team shut them down?"

Dr. Moore laughed. "It wasn't quite that exciting, but yes, they've been shut down."

"Tell them your news, Will," said Ma Etty, nudging Mr. Bridle.

"Oh, Etty," he drawled, "that's not news."

"Tell us!" everyone chorused.

The old cowboy drained his lemonade. "I don't like to gossip. I'm only telling you this so that if you run into Thomas around town, you can be nice to him."

The kids exploded with outrage.

"No way!" Bryce said, thudding his fist onto his thigh so hard he spilled his lemonade.

Mr. Bridle calmed them down just like he would a feisty mustang. "Jim Goodstein came over to apologize for Thomas. He had no idea the kind of trouble his grandson was getting into." Mr. Bridle paused. A wide smile spread across his face. "He asked my advice."

"Don't tell us you offered to take Thomas on at the ranch?" said Madison, looking horrified.

Ma Etty's laugh burbled out of her. "Oh, Willard, you didn't!"

He shook his head. " 'Course not, Etty. Summer's over." There was a long pause. "Maybe next year."

Ma Etty laughed again, and Paley shook her head. She wouldn't want to be stuck with Thomas for a whole summer, but then again, she'd felt that way about Bryce at first too, and now she couldn't imagine not seeing him every day. She watched him laughing with Leila near the lemonade cooler. His short, blond hair stuck up, making him look like a crazed porcupine, and his knuckles were scraped—not from fighting, but from moving heavy slabs of rock away from the dig zone.

She was going to miss him.

She was going to miss them all.

It wouldn't be easy back home. Her parents were planning to move her tricked-out computer into the family room, and there would be screen time restrictions. The new house rules included exercise every day and no skipping family mealtime.

Middle school was still middle school.

She had to decide if she would give the gaming club another try.

But there were good things too. Her mom had decided they should all learn to ski when winter rolled around, and Paley and Leila were thinking about joining the junior roller derby league in Denver. Best of all, the Bridles said she could come back any time she wanted to visit Prince.

Paley gazed over the excavation site to the lakeshore, where Prince and the other horses were nibbling wildflowers. As she watched him, it was hard to believe she'd been so obsessed with *Dragonfyre*. It was a cool game and all, but a pretend dragon was just that—pretend. What she'd learned from Prince was that she had to bring her best self to every situation.

And her best self meant her real self.

Not a cave troll.

Not the Blue Elf.

Just Paley.

ABOUT THE AUTHORS

KIERSI BURKHART grew up riding horses on the Colorado Front Range. At sixteen, she attended Lewis & Clark College in Portland and spent her young adult years in beautiful Oregon—until she discovered her sense of adventure was calling her elsewhere. Now she travels around with her best friend, a mutt named Baby, writing fiction for children of all ages.

AMBER J. KEYSER is happiest when she is in the wilderness with her family. Lucky for her, the rivers and forests of Central Oregon let her paddle, hike, ski, and ride horses right outside her front door. When she isn't adventuring, Amber writes fiction and nonfiction for young readers and goes running with her dog, Gilda.

ACKNOWLEDGMENTS

Huge thanks to Anna and the amazing team at Darby Creek; our rock star agent, Fiona Kenshole; horse expert, Heidi Siegel; the geology queen, Elaine Young; and the ever-brilliant Viva Scrivas. We are so lucky to have your help on the ranch!

A gelding named Red was the inspiration for Prince. Amber rode him on a pack trip in the Bob Marshall Wilderness of Montana when she was eleven years old. He was a big horse for a little girl, and he never ever let her down.